TINSEL & TEMPTATION

LEIGHTONSHIRE LOVERS
BOOK THREE

JONI HARPER

Cover design by Louise Brown.

Cover images @[Anna Subbotina] via Canva.com @[pixabay] via Canva.com

Please note: cover images are models and are not related to any characters in the story.

CAST

The Humans

In alphabetical order by last name

Mo Allen
Senior farrier at London International Horse Show.

Fernando Alma
Italian show jumper. As sweet as he is handsome.

Lady Patricia Babbington
Eccentric and generous. Eventing enthusiast. Jolly good sort.

Pippa Bell
Long-suffering groom to ill-tempered show jumper Doug Wallingford.

Fergus Bingley
Show jumper turned event rider. Known for absolute precision.

Joe Broughton

The UK's number one show jumping heart-throb.

Roger Broughton
Late father of Joe. Show jumping legend.

Zack Browne
Thirteen-year-old champion Shetland Pony Grand National rider.

Tom Clarke
Farmer whose land borders Templeton Manor. Boyfriend of Bunty Saunderton.

Ella Cooper
Up-and-coming show jumper. Competing in her first London International Horse Show.

Bill Dartmouth
Notorious horse dealer and trainer. User of unscrupulous methods.

Antonio de Luca
Italian show jumper. Sincere and kind-hearted.

Aimee Eastford
Number one-ranked British show jumper. Married to Patrick Ilmer.

Liberty Edwards
Runs a homemade luxury vegan candle company. Hattie's best friend. JaXX's girlfriend.

Eddie Flint

Daniel Templeton-Smith's kind-hearted head groom, engaged to Jenny Jackson.

Isabelle Francis
Twelve-year-old champion Shetland Pony Grand National rider.

Arnold T. Gladstone
American tech mogul, sponsor of the eventers vs show jumpers league competition at London International Horse Show.

Candice Gladstone
Wife of American tech mogul, thirty years his junior. A woman with motive.

Emma Holmer-Watson
Mid-ranked show jumper. Huge social media following.

Patrick Ilmer
Number two-ranked British show jumper. Married to Aimee Eastford.

Jenny Jackson
Local vet and amateur eventer, engaged to Eddie Flint.

JaXX
Reclusive singer-songwriter. Frontman of the Deciders. Lover of hats. Liberty Edward's boyfriend.

Wayne Jeffries
Local farrier. Mr March in the 'Rural Pleasures' charity calendar. Megan Taylor's boyfriend.

Harriet 'Hattie' Kimble

Horse whisperer. Event rider. Girlfriend of Daniel Templeton-Smith.

Gavin Ledbury
Part-time show jumper and full-time farmer.

Lucia Mason
Show jumper and social media star of #showjumpinghacks on Instagram.

Coraline Matthews
Farrier at London International Horse Show. TikTok sensation.

Holly Miller
Joe Broughton's head groom.

Fliss Moreton
Up-and-coming eventer, just joined the GB Young Rider team.

Helga Neilson
Greta Wolfe's blonde head groom.

Brian Norsley
Experienced farrier at London International Horse Show.

Imy Palmer-Drew
Scottish eventing star. Married to Kassie Palmer-Drew.

Kassie Palmer-Drew
Scottish artist. Married to Imy Palmer-Drew.

Clara Philips
Show jumping legend and daughter of famous show jumper Harvey Philips.

Henry Pottinger
Show jumper lothario. Petty and vindictive. Ex-boyfriend of Ella Cooper.

Bunty Saunderton
Daniel Templeton-Smith's yard hand and working pupil.

Otto Schneider
Olympic gold-winning show jumper. Very particular but fair.

Jonathan Scott
Medal-winning Australian rider. Known for vigorous pursuits.

Gerald Talbot
Private secretary to Lady Patricia. Loyal in every way.

Megan Taylor
Big dressage dreams. Now famous model. Girlfriend of Wayne Jefferies.

Daniel Templeton-Smith
Gorgeous and talented event rider. Owns Templeton Manor. Boyfriend of Hattie Kimble.

Doug Wallingford
Fifth-ranked British show jumper. A hard taskmaster with anger issues.

Greta Wolfe
Medal-winning German event rider.

The Animals

In alphabetical order

Arthur V
Sensitive young show jumping horse. Ridden and owned by Doug Wallingford.

Banyania XI
Antonio de Luca's young show jumping stallion.

Bright Spark III
Reliable show jumping stallion. Ridden by Doug Wallingford. Owned by B&F Electrical.

Captain Fury
Gavin Ledbury's chestnut gelding show jumper.

Club Garnett
Imy Palmer-Drew's chestnut gelding event horse.

Cookiesweet
Fernando Alma's dun gelding show jumper.

Dark Matter
Fliss Moreton's super-talented black event mare.

Dodger
Fergus Bingley's less-experienced Advanced horse.

Dynamite SM
Otto Schneider's top show jumping horse.

Eagle's Crest
Chestnut gelding. Ella Cooper's most experienced show jumper.

Gertrude

Daniel Templeton-Smith's small black cat – chief mouser of Templeton Manor.

Highland Daredevil
Shetland bay gelding, star of the Shetland Pony Grand National.

La Zanahoria
Fernando Alma's swift show jumping chestnut mare aka 'the carrot'.

Lipstick Lizzie
Shetland Pony Grand National contender.

Magical Mystery Meg
Shetland Pony Grand National contender.

Maximus IV
Otto Schneider's speed horse.

McQueen
Eddie Flint's swift three-legged collie. Proud rescue. Partial to pork scratchings.

Mermaid's Gold
A gift horse. 100% firecracker. Owned and ridden by Hattie Kimble.

MXA Royal Lion
Homebred chestnut mare ridden by Joe Broughton. Top speedster.

On-The-Up
Grey mare. Ella Cooper's less-experienced show jumper.

Pipplemouse
Skewbald gelding. Owned by Baroness Lathenby and ridden by Joe Broughton.

Pink Fizz
Roan gelding with talent and attitude. Owned and ridden by Daniel Templeton-Smith.

Poppet
Red male cocker spaniel puppy adopted by Hattie Kimble.

Popsy
Red female cocker spaniel puppy adopted by Jenny Jackson.

Purple Palace
Show jumping mare owned and ridden by Lucia Mason.

Rosalind
Fergus Bingley's championship-winning bay mare.

Salvadoro
Otto Schneider's piebald warmblood gelding. Owned by MWS GmbH.

Slinky
Ex-racehorse turned eventer owned by Daniel Templeton-Smith. Mermaid's Gold's field buddy.

Spicetown
Doug Wallingford's bay gelding show jumper.

Supersonic Bean
Chestnut gelding Shetland pony, star of the Shetland Pony Grand National.

The Rogue
Daniel Templeton-Smith's top event horse. Bold over fences. Fan of ginger biscuits.

Tiktac
Jonathan Scott's up-and-coming event horse.

Triple Threat
Greta Wolfe's less experienced event horse, owned by Mr & Mrs Schmidt.

Truckle Bay
Chunky bay gelding show jumper. Owned by Mr & Mrs Lemmington-Smythe and ridden by Joe Broughton.

Universal Pie
Smart piebald show jumping mare ridden by Clara Philips.

Washford Bay
Bright bay mare event horse. Owned and ridden by Greta Wolfe.

Westworlder
Event horse ridden by Greta Wolfe. Owned by Mrs Clifford.

Zippy Fantastic
Black show jumping mare ridden by Aimee Eastford and owned by TY Communications.

TUESDAY

CHAPTER ONE

DANIEL

Daniel Templeton-Smith hurries across the yard and up the lorry steps into the living area.

It's the week before Christmas. Usually at this time of year, all the horses aside from a few youngsters would be turned away for their winter holiday and Daniel would be doing more teaching and maybe a lecture demo or two. This year is different. He's been invited to compete in the eventers vs show jumpers league competition at this year's London International Horse Show. It's exciting. He's not been to the show since it switched from the old venue at Olympia to Excel, but he's heard great things about the setup.

He stows Hattie's and his suitcases into the small cupboard beside the door that serves as a wardrobe, and stocks the travel fridge with some food essentials – a container of milk plus a couple of bottles of wine, a pack of ham and a block of cheddar, some butter and a couple of microwave ready meals. He puts a couple of loaves of bread into one of the upper kitchen cabinets, along with a family pack of crisps, a multipack of Kit-Kats and several packets of ginger biscuits, which are exclusively for The Rogue. Daniel sees that there's already a bag of pasta and a jar of pasta sauce in the cupboard, so even if they can't find anywhere for dinner they've got a few options.

He makes sure there are a couple of tea towels in the under-sink cupboard, and that there's a stock of bottled water – just in case. Then he goes to the tiny shower room and double-checks the loo lid is down and the basin taps and shower are completely turned off and the towels are safely on the towel rails. He's just filled up the water tanks and he doesn't want an accident as they're driving down the motorway. He still remembers the time he left one of the basin taps on and the flood it created. It took weeks to get the room dry again.

New bedding is already on the double bed in the Luton over the cab, along with several extra blankets. It's been down to below freezing most nights this past week, and although it'll probably be a bit warmer in London than here in Leightonshire, Daniel doubts it'll be much above freezing. They do have a small electric radiator that can be switched on if they've got the suitcase generator running, or are hooked up to power, but it can be temperamental and it's better to have plenty of blankets just in case.

Before he goes to do the next job on his list, Daniel walks down the steps from the living area and opens the passenger side door. Climbing into the cab, he opens the glove compartment and checks, again, that he's packed The Rogue and Pink Fizz's passports. Without them, they won't be allowed onto the showground; that point was stressed multiple times during the online competitor's briefing a couple of weeks ago. It'd be gutting to drive all that way and then have to turn round and come back. But he doesn't need to worry. Just as they were the last time he checked, the passports are still in their plastic wallet in the glovebox along with another packet of ginger biscuits, a multipack of Polos, and a couple of Kit-Kats. Closing the glove box, he climbs back down out of the cab.

'Almost set?' asks Hattie as she puts a saddle into the tack locker in the side of the lorry and then removes two bridles from over her shoulder and hangs them beside the saddle.

'Almost,' says Daniel. Moving across to her, he reaches out and tucks a flyaway strand of Hattie's brown hair behind her ear. 'I just need to get the horses ready and we'll be good to go.'

'Fab,' she says, smiling as she goes on her tiptoes to give him a quick kiss. 'Your tack is loaded and I've got the rugs, stable equipment, feed and grooming kit and spare bucket on-board, so I'll head down to see Mermaid while you prep the horses.'

'Sounds good,' says Daniel.

He watches Hattie walk out of the yard and along the track towards the field where her diminutive event horse, Mermaid's Gold, and his own ex-racehorse, Slinky, are spending their winter holidays. In the distance, he can see that the two horses are standing at the field gate. Mermaid's Gold whinnies as her owner gets closer, and Daniel sees Hattie raise her hand and give the little chestnut mare a wave. He smiles. It's almost a year since Hattie moved Mermaid here and he can't imagine life without either of them now.

Hattie feeds the mare a Polo and strokes her muddy neck, then takes a few steps to the other side of the gate where Slinky is waiting hopefully for his Polo. Mermaid's Gold allows the much taller gelding to be given one Polo, then reverses towards him with her ears back, making it clear that he's had all he's getting and that she will not be sharing her human with him. Daniel chuckles. Mermaid's Gold might be barely fifteen hands high but she's absolutely the boss of the other horses.

Turning back towards the stables, Daniel thinks of the days ahead. He's looking forward to having a week away in London. It might not be a holiday as such, but a change is as good as a rest. With the rigours of the event season, they don't get much time for date nights or holidays, but with just two horses to look after and only one eventers vs show jumpers competition class running each day, they should have some downtime where they can go and see some of the sights and have dinner out a few times.

He heads towards The Rogue's stable. The tall bay gelding is looking out over the door, ears pricked.

'You know something's up, don't you?' says Daniel, grabbing the horse's travelling gear from outside the stable and taking it inside. 'I think you're going to enjoy it. You always like an audience and there'll be a big one in London.'

The Rogue blows out as if agreeing, then nuzzles Daniel's pocket, asking for a ginger biscuit. Daniel laughs, and fishes around in the pocket to find a quarter of a biscuit to feed him. The gelding munches it appreciatively.

Daniel fits the horse's all-in-one padded travel boots, which help protect his legs from any knocks while he's in the lorry, then puts on his tail bandage before fixing a padded poll guard to the headstall of The Rogue's leather headcollar. He's almost finished when Eddie, Daniel's long-time head groom, looks in over the stable door.

'How are you doing?' asks Eddie, pulling his beanie down further over his ginger hair to keep out the cold.

'Almost there,' replies Daniel. 'It feels weird heading off to a competition the week before Christmas.'

'I bet,' says Eddie, zipping up his puffa jacket. 'Shall I get Pink Fizz's gear on?'

'Please,' says Daniel. 'That'd be great.'

Once both horses are ready, Daniel loads them onto the lorry. The Rogue goes in first as he's the tallest and heaviest of the two. He walks up the ramp happily and immediately starts tucking into his haynet. Pink Fizz is on his toes as Daniel leads him from his stable and when he sees The Rogue already in the lorry, the roan gelding almost pulls Daniel over in his eagerness to load. Laughing, Daniel ties the horse up and watches as he also gets to work eating his haynet.

Hattie, back from seeing Mermaid's Gold, helps with the

ramp, and with both horses safely onboard, they walk across to the tack room where they find Bunty and Eddie cleaning tack. Despite the warmth coming from the plug-in electric radiator, Bunty, who always feels the cold acutely, still has her puffa jacket zipped up and her fluffy ear warmers on. Eddie has Poppet, Hattie's young cocker spaniel, sitting on his lap.

'We're heading out,' says Daniel as Hattie makes them two coffees to take on the road. 'Our arrival slot is booked for five and we don't want to be late and muck up their voyage control system.'

'Have an amazing time,' says Bunty, putting down her tack-cleaning sponge to hug Daniel and Hattie. 'We'll send you updates on the horses, and you must send us all the gossip from the show.'

Daniel laughs. 'Deal.'

'And don't worry about this little guy,' says Eddie, stroking Poppet. 'We'll take the best care of him.'

Hattie reaches out and strokes Poppet under his chin, his favourite place. She gives the spaniel a kiss on his silky head, then looks back at Eddie. 'Any problems, just let me know. I can be back here in a couple of hours and—'

'Of course, but we'll be fine,' says Eddie. He looks at Daniel. 'Make sure you beat those show jumpers.'

Daniel laughs. 'I'll give it my best shot.'

Leaving the warmth of the tack room, Daniel and Hattie carry their coffees across the yard and through the gate into the parking area. Through the half-open horse area windows, Daniel sees the horses are still contently munching their haynets.

Hattie and Daniel climb into the cab of the lorry and put the coffees into the cup holders on the dashboard. Hattie shivers. Despite all the layers they're wearing, it's cold inside the vehicle, and Daniel starts the engine and puts the heating on full to try and chase away the frigid air as fast as possible. As the engine fires into life, Daniel feels the familiar fizz of competition nerves in his stomach.

'You ready?' asks Hattie, smiling across at him from the passenger seat.

Daniel checks the glovebox once more, making sure the passports are inside, then smiles back, nodding. 'Let's do this.'

'This is going to be fun,' says Hattie.

Daniel agrees. But little does he know what lies in wait for him in London.

CHAPTER TWO

WAYNE

The setup at London International Horse Show is top notch, and Wayne Jefferies is stoked to be here. It's a real honour to have been picked as one of the show's on-site farriers and he's still pinching himself that he's made the cut. He's met the other farriers in the team – Mo and Brian, a couple of older blokes who've worked at the show for years, and Coraline, a thirtysomething like himself who's got a massive TikTok following. They seem a good bunch.

He's really looking forward to the week. The money is generous and he's got a dedicated space just a short distance from the stables to use as a forge. Plus his girlfriend, Megan Taylor, has come to London with him, so he's hoping they'll get some time to hang out as a couple. Things have been wild the past few months since they got together, what with him having a full farriery schedule and Megan getting signed as a model and almost immediately getting booked by a high-end luxury lingerie company for a massive campaign that's made her an instant household name. He's so proud of her and, if he's honest, he feels as if he's punching well above his weight as her boyfriend.

He's almost finished getting the forge organised. It hasn't

taken that long as the show has laid on a brand-new top-of-the-range furnace and anvil, so all he's had to do is unpack his other kit – hoof-cutters, hammers etc – and find them a home on the pegs and shelving supplied. Having unpacked and stored the last of his equipment, Wayne stands and takes a look at the space. This forge is far brighter than he's used to at his place back home, which will be helpful. It's also been well designed – the non-slip matting on the floor should be easy to keep clean, and the furnace seems to be efficiently flued, the extractor piping carrying the smoke up and out of the building. He's just considering whether to grab a quick cuppa when his phone beeps.

Pulling the device from his pocket, Wayne pushes his unruly mop of curly black hair from his eyes and reads the message from Megan:

> Daniel and Hattie are here. Plan is to meet at 6 in the Hand & Flower.

Smiling, Wayne types his reply:

> Great. See u there.

The Hand & Flower is an onsite pub for competitors, VIPs and those with backstage access. It's built alongside the viewing area and collecting ring for the international arena, with a long bar and a large, fake-grass beer garden with lots of seating. It's a big space, and although it seems kind of weird to him to have a pub garden inside, it's good to have the facility. Although the showground is huge, and there are multiple bar areas, once everyone's arrived and the show programme begins in earnest tomorrow, he has no doubt that this place will be rammed. But this evening, with only some of the competitors, grooms and crew onsite, it's busy but not packed out.

He scans the tables, looking for Megan and his mates. He recognises a few faces – show jumpers who look familiar but he can't remember their names, and Greta Wolfe the eventer, who's on a table with a couple of other people across the bar. There are a lot of tweedy-looking sorts, par for the course at this type of show, he guesses, and a big group of younger people wearing show crew sweatshirts.

Wayne finds Megan already seated at a table over on the far side of the pub garden area. Even dressed down in her leggings, oversized jumper and winter jacket with her long, dark brown hair tied up in a messy bun on the top of her head, she looks like a million dollars. Honestly, he feels like pinching himself every time he's with her. He's a hell of a lucky man.

As Megan stands up to greet him, Wayne can see a few of the blokes on the neighbouring table turning to stare at her. It doesn't bother him – it happens most places they go these days. The lingerie campaign has made her a familiar face to many, so it's pretty normal for people to ask for selfies and autographs.

Ignoring the guys watching, Wayne smiles at Megan and pulls her in for a kiss. She tastes like strawberries, as always.

'Hey you,' he says, kissing her on the tip of her nose.

'Hey,' replies Megan, smiling up at him. 'You're almost on time.'

Wayne laughs. Timekeeping is not his strong suit. 'I did my best.'

'There you are,' says Hattie. 'We thought you'd got lost.'

Giving Megan one last kiss, Wayne turns round to see Hattie and Daniel walking across the fake grass towards him. 'Sorry about that.'

'No worries,' says Daniel. 'We got champagne for the three of us and a beer for you. Is that all right?'

Wayne isn't keen on the fizzy wine stuff. He nods. 'That's perfect.'

Since Megan moved her dressage horse Velvet Mimosa to

Templeton Manor, the four of them have become good friends, and when Daniel's usual farrier retired a month back he asked Wayne to become the yard farrier too. It's always a pleasure working with nice people, and when you're mates already it's even better. Wayne can't believe how much his life has changed in the space of a year. At the beginning of the year, he was a regular bloke-about-town. Now he's happily settled in a relationship with a woman he adores and getting to do cool stuff like be an on-site farrier here at an international horse show.

As he and Megan sit down, Wayne sees the blokes on the nearby table have lost interest in staring and have returned to their own conversation. 'How was the journey for you?' he asks Daniel and Hattie.

'Pretty good,' says Daniel, pushing Wayne's pint across the table to him. 'We hit traffic as we got into London, but otherwise it was a fairly clear run.'

'Cool,' says Wayne, taking a sip of his beer. 'Where are you staying?'

'In the lorry,' replies Hattie, pouring the champagne into the three glasses. 'We could have got a hotel but they're all pretty pricy, so as we've got the lorry here anyway we thought we may as well use it.'

'It's going to be weird without the dog though,' says Daniel. 'I'm so used to Poppet commandeering most of the bed and forcing us into a small strip along one side that I'm not sure what I'm going to do with all the space.'

'I'm sure you'll think of something,' says Megan, smirking.

Hattie laughs.

'What about you guys?' asks Daniel.

'We're in the closest hotel,' says Megan. 'It's nice, and means Wayne's nearby if someone needs a shoe sorted urgently.'

Hattie gives a glass of champagne to Megan and Daniel, then raises her own in a toast. 'It's great to be here. Here's to a fun and successful week.'

Megan and Daniel raise their glasses to clink Hattie's.

Wayne lifts his pint and does the same. 'To a brilliant week.'

They all drink. As Wayne takes a second mouthful of beer, he feels excitement and nerves mingling in his stomach. They're not about being a farrier at the show, but something different. Because Wayne has a secret. It's something he's been planning for more than a month. Something important. Something romantic.

Something that could change his life forever.

WEDNESDAY

CHAPTER THREE

ELLA

This is really happening. Ella Cooper can't quite believe it.

She's dreamt about competing at London International Horse Show ever since she was a tiny tot on the leading rein, and this year she's actually done it. She's here and entered into all the main show jumping classes.

It still doesn't feel real. All those years begging riding lessons in return for working at the local horse stables, then doing paper rounds before school and pot washing in the local pub after school, to save up enough money to, years later, buy herself a horse, have paid off. She's so grateful to her parents for helping her out where they could; without them, this wouldn't be possible. When they saw how determined she was, and that she had some raw talent, they supported her in any way they could. They don't have a lot of money, but Mum even learnt about stable management and handling horses on the ground, so when Ella managed to get a bank loan to start a yard of her own, Mum became her part-time groom.

Over the arena speakers, calming classical music is playing. The acclimatisation sessions are to let horses and riders get familiar with the international arena before the grandstands are full and the pressure of competition is on. Ella's grateful for the opportunity – it's good to have the chance to get her bearings without the spotlight being on them, and she's sure that after the long journey here yesterday and a night in his new stable, her horse is thankful for the opportunity to stretch his legs.

As she rides around the international arena, Ella feels like she might burst with excitement. She's here. She's finally here!

But Ella knows this is the calm before the storm – in just a few hours, the show will open its doors to the public and the now-empty grandstand seating all around the arena will be filled with spectators. Out in the collecting ring, there are tractor trailers loaded with brightly coloured jumps which, once this last acclimatisation session and this morning's FEI Dressage World Cup class are finished, will be brought into the arena and set up for the first show jumping competition of the week. The tension and anticipation already feel almost tangible, and Ella knows they're only going to increase.

As her horse trots relaxed circles, Ella takes a look at the other riders. Honestly, the names of the people acclimatising their horses to the arena during this session would read like a who's who of the horse world. Across the arena, she sees this year's Badminton champion, Daniel Templeton-Smith, and his star horse, The Rogue. Near to him, there's the current show jumping individual Olympic gold medallist – Otto Schneider – riding his top horse Dynamite SM. Closer to where Ella's riding, she sees two of the Italian Olympic show jumping team and the Japanese rider who won individual bronze at the Olympics. Down the other end of the space are Aimee Eastford and Patrick Ilmer – the two top-ranked British show jumping riders – loosening up their horses, and Doug Wallingford – ranked fifth in the UK – who seems to be having a tricky time on a massive grey horse that's taken a dislike to the digital advertising boards that line the arena's edge.

The horse Ella is riding, Eagle's Crest, is the more experienced of the two horses she's brought with her. Originally she'd been meant to ride three here, but the third was Evergreen – a horse owned by Henry Pottinger. Ella shudders. She doesn't want to think about Henry, or the nightmare he's become. Because Henry is her ex and also a show jumper. He should be riding here at the London International Horse Show this week, but a recent shoulder injury has prevented him from competing, thankfully.

They split up a couple of months ago, but he's still angry about it. He blames her for their breakup because she was the one who ended things, but *he* had been the one to cheat on her with at least two other women. Ella saw the naked pictures of the three of them together on his phone, and he didn't deny what he'd done when she challenged him. He told her it was a one off and it'd never happen again, but she didn't believe him. There'd been hints before that he'd been messing her around – lipstick marks on his white competition shirts when he came back from shows, hushed phone calls in the middle of the night to who knows who when he thought she was asleep, texts from women she's never heard of or met. Henry's a fuckboy. She'd always known it really, but for a long while he'd managed to gaslight her into believing he actually did love her.

But he never did, she's 100% sure of that. In fact, she believes that the only reason Henry's still angry about their breakup is because she was the instigator. Apparently he'd never been dumped before and it wounded his pride. She shakes her head at the ridiculousness of it. Even though he never liked riding Evergreen – saying the horse didn't have enough firepower for him – he still, predictably, took Evergreen away from her after she'd told him it was over between them.

Ella misses that horse far more than she misses Henry.

Anyway, she doesn't want to think about bloody Henry the cheater, not now and not ever again. She needs to concentrate on the show and her horses. Popping Eagle's Crest into canter, they do a few easy circles then come down over the high cross pole practice fence. The chestnut gelding pops the jump happily.

'Good boy,' says Ella, rubbing the horse's powerful neck.

She pilots him around a U-shape turn and they approach an upright fence of about three foot six – she was trained in feet and inches and always struggles with the conversion to centimetres. Again, Eagle's Crest pops it with ease.

Smiling, Ella brings the gelding back to a walk and lets him have a long rein to stretch out his neck. He's feeling good and there's no sense in overdoing things this morning. Their first class of the show – the Christmas Pudding Stakes – takes place this afternoon so she doesn't want to do too much this morning. The show runs from Wednesday to Sunday and it's a pretty intense schedule, especially with just two horses. She's not competing in every show jumping class as she doesn't want to overwork them, but it's important not to tire Eagle's Crest before they've even begun.

After walking the horse off for a few circuits of the massive arena, and doing a bit more equestrian star-studded people watching, Ella dismounts in the collecting ring, loosens the chestnut gelding's girth and runs up the stirrups, then leads Eagle's Crest back along the horse walk to the stables. Her two allocated stables are towards the end of the third row, and as she and Eagle's Crest approach, the pretty grey face of her second horse, On-The-Up, looks over the stable door, a wisp of hay in her mouth. The grey mare pricks up her ears and whickers as she sees her stablemate returning. Eagle's Crest whinnies back, even though he usually isn't super keen on his younger stablemate when they're at home.

Opening the door to his stable, Ella leads Eagle's Crest inside. The frosty weather means that even inside it's a bit chilly, so she throws the horse's Thermatex rug over his quarters to stop him getting cold.

Taking off her riding hat, Ella sets it down outside, runs her fingers through her short bobbed blonde hair so it's not sticking to her skin, then pulls on her woolly hat. Returning to the stable, she starts to untack Eagle's Crest. Usually her mum helps her out at competitions but this week is different. Cash has been tight of late due to a major storm the previous month causing significant damage. The stables had to be reroofed and it wasn't a cost she'd budgeted for, so she really couldn't afford to pay a freelance groom to do the yard at home this week. Instead, Mum has stayed behind looking after the yard and the younger horses. It's the right choice, Ella knows that. It's just that she'd never expected to feel so alone here without her.

Making sure the horse is rugged warmly and has everything he needs – water, hay and his snack-a-ball filled with his favourite treats – Ella gives Eagle's Crest and On-The-Up a herbal horse treat and a kiss on the nose each, then carries her tack and riding hat back to her lorry.

As she walks, she feels her phone vibrate in her pocket. *That's probably Mum wondering how things are going,* thinks Ella. *I need to send her an update.*

Once she's reached her lorry, Ella loads the tack into the locker on the side, and puts her hat into her hat carrier, then locks the storage locker and heads up the steps to the living area. It's a basic horsebox with a compact living area, but with just her there's more than enough room to stay here comfortably. Switching the travel kettle on, Ella pulls out her phone and reads the messages.

Her breath catches in her throat.

WHY ARE YOU COMPETING AT LIHS?????

YOU'RE GOING TO BE OUT-CLASSED STUPID COW.

YOU'RE SHIT. YOU KNOW THAT RIGHT????

YOU DON'T BELONG IN SHOW JUMPING.

REMEMBER THOSE NAKED PICS YOU SENT ME FOR MY BIRTHDAY? IF YOU DON'T PULL OUT OF THE SHOW I'LL SEND THEM TO THE GUYS – THEY'LL HAVE A LAUGH AT YOU NAKED.

THAT'LL SERVE YOU RIGHT YOU BITCH.

WITHDRAW NOW!!

Ella's hands tremble. She feels as if she's going to be sick.

It's an unknown number, but she knows exactly who's behind the messages.

Why is he doing this? *He* was the one who cheated, not her.

Ella blocks the number and deletes the messages, but she knows it's futile. He'll just get another SIM or burner phone and message her on another new number, just as he has done so many times already. He tells her repeatedly that she's nothing, that she's shit, but he still won't leave her alone.

Ella bites her lip, trying not to cry. Would Henry really send those pictures to his show jumping mates? She can't withdraw from competing here at London International, she's dreamt about this moment for so long, and if she pulls out now without a proper excuse she might never get invited back. It could set back her show jumping career years.

She has to risk it. She cannot withdraw; she just can't.

But the thought of Henry following through on his threat, and his show jumping friends seeing her naked, makes her suddenly sick to her stomach. She rushes to the tiny loo, drops to her knees and vomits until there's nothing left.

Why is he doing this to her? Why can't he just leave her alone?

Her head starts to pound, a stress headache spreading across her forehead. Getting up, Ella flushes the loo and cleans her teeth. She moves back into the horsebox's living area and takes a few sips of water. It doesn't help her feel any better.

This can't be happening.

Anxiety builds in her chest. Ella wishes she could talk to someone but she doesn't want to call Mum and worry her. She needs to handle this herself; she just wishes she knew how to stop Henry harassing her. She's asked him before, so many times, but he pays no notice.

As the tears stream down her cheeks, Ella opens the cupboard above the sink and pulls out an old bottle of gin. She isn't usually much of a drinker but – if she's going to hold her nerve, knowing that as soon as Henry sees her competing on camera, or one of his mates tells him that she is, he'll send the nudes – she needs something to help take the edge off, to numb the embarrassment. Just enough for her to compete.

Unscrewing the top, she takes a long slug of gin from the bottle.

Yuck.

Her throat feels like it's on fire. She can't help but cough. Her eyes are watering from the taste, but she grimaces and has another big mouthful and then another.

She just wants to make Henry and his threat go away.

CHAPTER FOUR

HATTIE

The shopping village really is something else. Everything and anything horse- and pony-related is on sale here – from tack to rugs, clothing to art, and rocking horses to horseboxes. The show's doors only opened half an hour ago and already the place is packed with people. There are Christmas songs playing over the speakers, and many of the stands are dressed with tinsel and lights. Everything feels very festive.

It's been years since Hattie came to this show. It was held in a different part of London then, at Olympia, and she must have been about ten years old. Mum had taken on some extra yard work to save the money, and they'd taken the train early in the morning to London, arriving right at the moment the show opened. It had been like nothing Hattie had ever imagined and it all seemed impossibly glamorous. From the show jumpers, who she'd only seen in magazines or on the telly before, to the children her age galloping around the arena in the Shetland Grand National, and the Household Cavalry with their daring feats of bareback riding and jumping through rings of fire. When the end of the performance came, and the show finale was performed with Santa and fake snow and carols, the whole thing had seemed magical.

She smiles at the memory and the warm feeling of nostalgia that comes with it, but underneath the fondness there's a pang of grief too. Mum would've loved to have been here this week, watching Daniel compete and sharing the experience with them. Hattie shakes her head. It's been two years now since she lost her mum but she doesn't think the sadness will ever go.

A person walking past knocks Hattie's arm with a large shopping bag slung over their shoulder. The impact pulls Hattie from her memory.

'I'm sorry,' says the woman, glancing round.

'It's okay,' Hattie replies.

The memory is gone again and Hattie focuses back on the job in hand. She's not looking for much, just a pair of socks. She thought she'd packed everything she needed, but it seems she forgot to include any socks. They're probably still sitting on the bed back at Templeton Manor, but they're not much use to her there. At least there's plenty of choice here in the shopping village. Maybe too much choice.

Hattie browses some pony print socks at an equestrian accessories stand that are prettier than her usual plain black ones but double the price she'd usually pay, so she decides to keep looking and heads back out onto the main concourse.

She's moving away from the stand when she suddenly gets the strangest feeling. It's as if she's being stared at. Shivering, Hattie looks round. There are hordes of people all around her but no one seems to be interested in her – they're all walking along, their attention either on the people they're with or the stands that line the walkway.

Weird.

Shrugging off the feeling, Hattie continues on between the stands until she reaches a saddlery store. She ducks inside and makes her way to the equestrian clothing section. They have some lovely boot socks, which are perfect for this week, but sadly nothing in her size. Empty-handed, Hattie leaves and heads towards a country fashion stand she can see up towards the end of the walkway. Maybe they'll have something suitable.

As she walks, Hattie passes a rocking horse display. There are ten of the most gorgeous hand-carved and hand-painted rocking horses she's ever seen, each big enough for an adult to ride. Hattie smiles, thinking how much fun they are, although the price is pretty eye-watering. There are greys, bays and a chestnut with a flaxen mane and tail that reminds her of Mermaid's Gold.

It's only been a day but she really misses Mermaid. This is the first time since Badminton back in May that she's left her for more than a day and it feels so strange not to be heading down to the mare's field, feeding her and checking her over, then giving her her favourite treat, a Polo. It's odd not to have Poppet with her too. Since he came into her life, he's been like her constant shadow. Feeling a pang of homesickness, Hattie pulls out her phone and calls Eddie.

He answers after three rings. 'Everything okay?'

'I was just about to ask you the same thing,' replies Hattie, stepping to the side of the walkway to avoid causing a jam in the flow of shoppers.

'All's good here. Mermaid's happy in her field, I've just taken her and Slinky some hay as it was another hard frost last night, and Poppet is having a high old time running around the yard with McQueen. From the look on his face, I reckon McQueen is probably having less fun.'

Hattie laughs. 'Poor McQueen, and thank you. It's just weird being away from them.'

'I bet,' says Eddie. 'And no problem. We're all rooting for the eventers in the competition. Send us an update after the comp today.'

'Will do, and thanks again,' says Hattie, ending the call.

As she puts her phone back in her pocket, suddenly she shivers. There's that feeling again as if someone is watching her, staring at her from behind.

She turns to look, but can't see anyone looking obviously in her direction. It's busy all around her. There's a group of kids chattering about the upcoming Shetland Pony Grand National heat, a bunch of mums with buggies and little children, a loved-up couple walking hand in hand, and lots of people in pairs or larger groups laden down with shopping bags. No one seems to be paying Hattie any attention.

It's strange, though. She doesn't usually get this sort of feeling in crowds. Telling herself she must be imagining it, Hattie continues on along the walkway towards the clothing stand and tries to put the feeling from her mind. But however hard she tries, she fails.

She just can't shake the creepy feeling that someone here *is* watching her.

CHAPTER FIVE

ELLA

'Competitors may now walk the course for the Christmas Pudding Stakes,' announces the commentator over the collecting ring loudspeaker. 'The course will be open for walking for fifteen minutes.'

As the big red curtains to the international arena open to let the competitors through, Ella gets her first glimpse of the course. Her first thought is that it looks big but eminently jumpable. Her second is that she's going to be sick.

Swallowing down the nausea, she follows the other competitors into the hallowed arena. The lights are so bright, they make her blink, and she loses her footing and teeters for a moment, almost falling, but she manages to grab for the digital arena board, which helps her regain her balance and stay upright.

There are already a lot of spectators in their seats, keenly watching the course walk. They peer down at the competitors from the grandstands, looking for their favourites. Ella isn't a big name – she knows no one will be looking for her – so she tries to ignore them and focus on the fences, but it's hard when your vision is a bit blurred and you're feeling more than a little dizzy.

Damn that gin.

Ella never usually drinks – the gin is her mum's, who likes a celebratory gin and tonic after they've had a good day at a show. Ella has never much liked the taste of alcohol or the sensation of being drunk. Why the hell did she drink that gin earlier? And why did she drink so much of it? It was a foolish move. Self-sabotaging.

Bloody Henry.

As she paces out the related distance between a red-and-white vertical with a hanging filler in the shape of a Christmas cracker, and a red-and-yellow oxer with cartoon snowmen attached to the wings, Ella has a quick glance round at the other competitors. Henry knows a lot of these people – has he asked them if she's walking the course? Have they already confirmed she is? Has he sent the photos? Are his mates secretly laughing at her?

Oh no.

Ella loses her footing again. She staggers forward.

'Are you okay?' asks Antonio de Luca, a super attractive Italian rider, as he reaches out to grab her arm, holding her upright.

'Yes I'm... Thank you,' she says, her cheeks reddening.

'It's okay,' replies Antonio, his expression one of concern. 'Are you sure you're feeling okay?'

'Yes, thanks,' says Ella, moving quickly away from Antonio and hurrying on with her course walk. But she's not okay at all. She's not taking in any of the fences properly and she's already forgotten the number of strides in the related distance.

What's wrong with me?

It's the gin. She knows it. She's been such an idiot. There's no way she can jump in this state. There's no way she's safe to ride when she can't even walk in a straight line properly. She can't risk her horses.

I'm going to have to withdraw.

With her mind made up, Ella turns back towards the exit to

the collecting ring. Her stomach lurches and she thinks she's going to vomit. Quickly, she hurries across the arena towards the exit. It feels as if the audience and her fellow competitors are watching her, that they can tell she's drunk.

I need to get out of here.

Ella's vision starts blurring. Black spots dance across her eyes.

The nausea keeps rising.

The lights are so bright, they're almost blinding.

The whole arena seems as if it's spinning around her, a kaleidoscope of spectators, competitors and brightly coloured fences.

This is bad.

Ella stumbles forward. She has to get to the exit. She can't vomit in the international arena. She just can't. She'd never live it down. And what if the TV cameras capture it? Or one or more of the spectators film it and put it on TikTok or Insta? It can't happen. She walks faster, breaks into a jog, her eyes fixed on the exit, desperate to reach it.

She never even sees the Christmas display. The three larger-than-life penguins wearing Santa hats are positioned around a six-foot-long and three-foot-wide shallow pool that will double as a water tray in future classes. Floating in the water are several yellow rubber ducks wearing little Santa outfits, and around the edge of the pool are boxes wrapped in Christmas paper.

Ella stumbles into them. The gifts are sent flying as she loses her balance, tripping over a particularly large gift. She cries out as she topples forward, unable to stop her momentum, and falls face-first, landing with a loud splash in the pool. Presents and Santa ducks scatter all around her. A couple of the ducks are trapped beneath Ella, digging hard into her ribs and knocking the breath from her lungs. The water's cold – icy cold. She feels immediately sober.

Oh my God. This is a nightmare.

Spluttering, Ella flails around, trying to get herself upright. She grabs the nearest penguins to help pull herself up, but it doesn't work. The penguins look solid but they're made of hollow fibreglass so there's not much weight to them. All grabbing them does is topple the two largest penguins down on top of her in the water.

She hears laughter from somewhere above her in the grandstands. A young child asks their parent why the lady is hurting the penguins; another asks why she's trying to swim in the pond.

Ella curses under her breath as she desperately tries to get onto her hands and knees. Water sloshes out of the trays and onto the synthetic sand. The final penguin standing falls onto her, its happy smile taunting her. Mocking her. She's never felt more embarrassed.

I have to get out of here.

'Let me help,' says a male voice.

Looking up, Ella sees Joe Broughton – the hottest show jumper in the UK, both in terms of competition form and looks – gazing down at her with a kind expression. He holds out his hand and, although she's almost dying of embarrassment, Ella takes it, letting him pull her to her feet and out of the water.

'What happened?' he asks, his eyes filled with concern.

Ella blushes, her cheeks feeling as if they're on fire. She shakes her head. 'I don't know. A funny turn or something.'

'Are you okay to ride?' says Joe.

'No, I don't think so. I'm going to withdraw.'

'Can I help you back to the collecting ring?' asks Joe. 'You look really pale. Maybe you should have the medics check you out.'

'I'll be fine, but thanks.' Ella forces a smile. There's no way she wants the medics to look at her and tell the show organisers that she's drunk. 'And thanks again for helping me.'

'You're welcome,' says Joe.

'Good luck in the class,' Ella adds, as she squelches back towards the exit.

She doesn't see Joe standing and watching her until she's safely out of the arena and back in the collecting ring. Ella also doesn't see the many phones that have been recording the incident, but she knows that they will have been. Everything is filmed these days, so she knows that the footage will already be on social media, and she cringes at the thought of it. But it's done now. She can't change it. She's just going to have to brazen it out.

Apologising to the ground crew, who are heading into the arena to rearrange the trashed penguin display, Ella tells the collecting ring stewards that she's withdrawing from the Christmas Pudding Stakes as she's feeling really unwell. They radio her withdrawal through to the show office, and cross her number off the whiteboard where the jumping order is displayed.

Ella feels a wave of sadness washing over her.

Today was supposed to be a great day. It was meant to be the highlight of her year – making everything she's worked for all these years come to fruition. Instead she's made a fool of herself and blown the first day at the show she's wanted to compete at ever since she was a little kid.

Henry's won.

I've let myself down. I've let the horses down. And I've let my parents down.

Ella heads back to her horsebox – and cries.

CHAPTER SIX

JOE

'And next up in the Christmas Pudding Stakes we have Joe Broughton riding Mr & Mrs Lemmington-Smythe's Truckle Bay,' announces the commentator.

As the red curtains open and Joe rides his chunky bay gelding through into the international arena, the crowd applauds and he can hear girls calling his name. This kind of reception is usual for him these days, but he still can't get used to it. And it's not just here at the shows; when he's home training, he receives stacks of fan mail and emails, and loads of DMs on his socials. He knows it's what's landed him the big sponsorship deals, but sometimes he yearns for the days when no one knew him and he could just focus on the jumping.

As the buzzer sounds, Joe asks Truckle Bay to take a few steps backwards. Truck obliges, although a swish of the tail tells Joe the bay horse is keen to get to work. Joe salutes to the judges, and then puts the gelding into canter. Truck bounces eagerly forward, ready for action.

The Christmas Pudding Stakes is a one-round speed class, and as Joe was one of the last numbers to be drawn he's had the advantage of watching how the course has been riding. It's been causing its fair share of problems – notably the planks at six, and the final combination are where the majority of the faults have been incurred. Joe hopes the strategy he's devised will help him go clear.

They start off well. Truckle Bay makes a careful jump over the first fence, a yellow-and-white oxer heading away from the entrance to the arena, then moves swiftly on to the London Bus fence at two – the upright 'bus' painted onto a solid hanging filler. Joe asks the bay to take a tight turn back to the spread fence at three with the glittery snowball filler, and he responds well, staying balanced and in rhythm around the turn and clearing the spread effortlessly. He asks the bay to steady before they turn into the red-and-white vertical with a Christmas cracker hanging filler, and make light work of it before accelerating to get in four big strides through a dog-leg turn to a red-and-yellow oxer with cartoon snowmen on the wings.

So far, so good.

Fence six, the planks, is next, and Joe makes sure the gelding doesn't put in one of his trademark 'flyers' at the unforgiving fence. Truckle Bay leaps over the planks with a foot to spare, then Joe pushes him on, and he lengthens his stride down to a large spread with Christmas trees beneath the poles. Joe does a quick half-halt to make sure the gelding is back on his hocks to jump the vertical with wings in the shape of Big Ben, and they leap over easily.

Nearly done.

He hears murmurs from the audience, a smattering of applause. But it's not over yet. There's still the final combination to go – a treble with a maximum-height vertical, one stride to a maximum-height oxer, then two strides to a second maximum-height oxer. Under each of the fences are huge Christmas presents wrapped in shiny red-and-green paper, matching the red-and-green poles. Some horses earlier in the class spooked at the light reflecting off the shiny paper. Joe hopes Truck won't let it bother him.

They keep moving forward around the turn and Joe sees a good stride into the first element of the combination. The bay horse's ears flick forward, focused on the fence. He pops over the first fence and easily makes the stride to the second element, but as the bay gelding lands he stumbles.

The crowd gasp.

Joe sits up, letting the horse reestablish his stride. Luckily Truck recovers quickly, but they're now a long way off from the third element and their momentum is lost. The distance should be two big strides, but Joe makes a snap decision and holds the gelding for three. It's a hugely risky move – if the horse gets too deep to the fence, he won't be able to get clear of the front poles.

The audience is silent as they hold their breath.

'You've got this, boy,' says Joe, under his breath.

Truckle Bay takes the short three strides and leaps steeply into the air over the final element. For a moment, it's as if horse and rider are frozen in time, mid-air. Then they land on the other side. Joe looks behind them – the fence is still up. They're clear.

The crowd cheers.

Joe rubs the gelding's neck, telling him, 'Clever boy, what a star.'

Truckle Bay snorts, as if acknowledging that he is indeed extremely clever and a star, and puts in a cheeky spook at the penguin water feature. Joe laughs and holds the gelding straight as they gallop towards the finish line where the clock will be stopped. But as he does, he's suddenly not thinking about the finish or their time or where they've come in the class rankings. Instead, his thoughts skip back to the woman – Ella – who fell into the water feature during the course walk. Poor her. She seemed so upset. Joe really hopes she's okay.

Next moment, Truckle Bay gallops through the finish. The

crowd whoops and applauds. A group of teenagers in the front row scream his name and wave 'I heart Joe' banners. Slowing Truck to a walk, Joe gives the horse a long rein and another rub on the neck, then waves to the crowd. 'Thank you.'

The applause intensifies.

As Joe and Truckle Bay leave the arena, the commentator announces, 'And that's Joe Broughton on Truckle Bay going into the lead with a fifteen-second advantage, with just two more horses to jump in the class.'

Joe hopes they've done enough to keep the lead.

He doesn't need to worry. They win the class with their fifteen-second lead, the last two competitors having a fence down each in their pursuit of an even faster time.

Winning is always a great feeling, and to have an early win under your belt on the first day of a five-day show like this is a real confidence boost. As the prize winners line up in the international arena, Joe manoeuvres Truckle Bay into the top spot. He congratulates Antonio de Luca, who is beside him in the line-up in second place, and smiles congratulations to Aimee Eastford in third and Otto Schneider in fourth.

The sponsors of the Christmas Pudding Stakes – a well-known champagne brand – present the rosettes and prizes, and Joe and Truckle Bay pose for photographs with them, the bay gelding proudly wearing his red rosette on his breastplate, the winner's sash and the winner's rug, and Joe holding the trophy. Once all the competitors down to tenth have been presented with their prizes, Joe and Truckle Bay lead the victory lap around the arena.

This is Truck's favourite part.

'Steady, mate,' says Joe, trying to stop the gelding going too fast.

The band plays. The crowd cheers. People are chanting their names. The banners with 'I heart Joe' and 'Kiss me Joe' and 'Pick me Joe' are being waved by more teenagers than he can count. As Truck maintains his pace, Joe grins up at the stands and blows a few kisses, prompting even louder screams from a group of five teenagers – four girls and a guy – who are almost hanging over the barrier as he canters past.

After one lap, the other horses and riders peel off and exit through the red curtains. Only Joe and Truckle Bay remain – it's time for them to take their solo lap of honour. Usually this is the best bit. The feeling of winning, the joyful pride in his bay gelding's stride, and the cheering of the crowd combines into the most amazing rush.

But as the lights are dimmed, and Joe finally lets Truck lengthen his stride as they canter down the long side towards the exit with the spotlight illuminating their path, there's something, someone, who Joe just can't shake from his mind.

Ella.

CHAPTER SEVEN

DANIEL

It's neck and neck in the first round of the eventers vs show jumpers league competition, and Daniel's next to jump. The teams are made up of six riders who will battle it out each day over a different show jumping track. The winners of the league competition will be the team with the lowest penalty points at the end of the last jumping round on Saturday.

The teams are a virtual who's who of eventing and show jumping talent, and Daniel can hardly believe he's here. On the eventer's side with him are German event team stalwart Greta Wolfe, show jumper turned eventer Fergus Bingley, Scottish eventing star Imy Palmer-Drew, Australian eventer Jonathan Scott, and up-and-coming young rider team sensation Fliss Moreton. It's a strong team, Daniel thinks, but the show jumpers are equally accomplished, with Antonio de Luca, Clara Philips, Fernando Alma, Emma Holmer-Watson, Doug Wallingford and Joe Broughton on the team, and here at the London International Horse Show they're on home turf.

'Greta's clear,' says Hattie to Daniel as he and The Rogue come to a halt beside where she's standing at the side of the warmup arena. 'So are Fergus and Imy.'

'Jonathan told me he'd had a fence down.'

Hattie nods. 'Yeah, at those orange fillers which have been causing all the trouble. The show jumpers have fared the same. It's down to you and Fliss to win it.'

'No pressure then,' says Daniel, as light-heartedly as he can manage because, if he's honest, he's really feeling it. Jumping here in the enclosed, pressure-cooker environment of the International Arena is a far cry from the rolling countryside of Badminton. The warmup area is a lot smaller than they're used to as well, but at least it isn't too busy – with only Fliss Moreton, Doug Wallingford and himself to jump.

As if sensing his nerves, Hattie reaches out and gives Daniel's leg a squeeze. She gives him a reassuring smile. 'You've got this.'

The Rogue shakes his head and blows out, as if to say the course and the atmosphere is nothing they can't handle.

Daniel strokes the big bay gelding's neck and smiles at Hattie. 'Thanks. I just want it to go well this week. Greta told me earlier that if the audience enjoys the competition, it could become an annual thing.'

The collecting ring steward calls his name, beckoning him across.

'Here goes,' says Daniel to Hattie.

'Good luck,' says Hattie. 'And don't forget to have fun.'

'We'll do our best,' replies Daniel, riding forward towards the steward and the entrance to the arena.

As they get closer, he hears applause and the commentator announcing, 'And that's a clear round for Fernando Alma and La Zanahoria, with just three more horses to jump.'

Daniel can't help but smile at the chestnut mare's name – Carrot – but Fernando's clear has put even more pressure on him and The Rogue to jump clear. As the steward waves them forward into the arena, Daniel gives The Rogue's neck a rub and then asks him to walk through the big red curtains.

Wow.

It's so bright inside the arena, it makes him blink. With the brightness, the noise of the audience still clapping the departing Fernando and La Zanahoria, and the electronic advertising boards around the edge of the arena flashing up their adverts, Daniel feels momentarily disorientated. He longs for the green turf of an eventing show jumping arena.

The Rogue, on the other hand, loves a crowd. Arching his neck, he seems to grow a few inches taller as he marches into the arena, enjoying the applause. Daniel laughs, and in that moment his nerves disappear. The bell sounds for them to start and as Daniel salutes the judges, the audience falls silent.

Popping The Rogue into canter, they begin. The first few fences are big – a couple of inches higher than the full height show jumping track at Badminton – but straightforward. The Rogue is enjoying himself. He jumps happily through the treble, over the oxer with a large water tray beneath it, and flies the two steeplechase-esque brush fences, then continues on to the double where he takes a huge leap over the brightly painted Christmas Cracker filler under the second element, snorting in mid-air to the delight of the crowd, and sailing around the course to the final fence. This is the one that's been causing trouble to a few of the riders – an entirely orange fence with a filler in the shape of three huge oranges.

As they make the turn, The Rogue snorts again. The crowd titters, but this time Daniel feels the big bay hesitate. Pushing him forward, Daniel tells the gelding, 'It's okay, it's just orange.'

With another, louder snort, the horse accelerates forward and does a massive leap over the fence, clearing it by at least a foot. They land, clear, and as Daniel rubs The Rogue's neck and tells the gelding over and over how clever he is, the audience cheer and clap.

'And that's an excellent clear round from Daniel Templeton-Smith and a rather vocal The Rogue,' says the commentator in a jovial manner. 'The score is level between the eventers and the show jumpers with just the last two riders now to jump.'

As Doug Wallingford and his young grey gelding, Arthur V, enter the arena, Daniel rides out to the collecting ring.

Hattie rushes up to meet him. 'That was fantastic,' she says, pulling a piece of ginger biscuit from her pocket and feeding it to the expectant Rogue. 'And what a massive jump he did over that last fence.'

'I know,' says Daniel, grinning. 'Maybe he missed his calling and should've been a show jumper.'

The Rogue blows out hard, as if to say he can do anything, then nudges Hattie's pocket for some more ginger biscuit.

Laughing, Hattie feeds the gelding another piece. 'You know how clever you are, don't you, Rogue.'

'He totally does,' says Daniel, dismounting and throwing the Thermatex rug Hattie hands him over the gelding to keep him warm while they wait for the results. In the corner of the collecting area, the arena crew are bringing a trailer packed with dog agility equipment closer to the entrance of the international arena, getting ready for the next class on the schedule.

'Well done,' says Fliss Moreton, riding past on her black mare, Dark Matter. She's the last competitor in the warmup now and will be the final person in the competition to jump. 'I hope I can do a decent round for the team.'

Poor Fliss, thinks Daniel. Just barely nineteen and newly invited onto the Young Rider Squad, she looks terrified. 'You'll be okay. All you need to do is get round.'

'Okay,' says Fliss, her teeth chattering from nerves. 'It's just so different here.'

'It is, but remember, it's meant to be fun,' adds Daniel. 'And Dark Matter's a star.'

Fliss gives a tight smile. 'I'll try.'

'Good luck,' says Hattie.

Fliss's smile widens just slightly. 'Thanks.'

As Fliss and Dark Matter continue on towards the entrance, Hattie feeds The Rogue another piece of ginger biscuit and asks Daniel, 'Shall I walk him round while you see how the last two jump?'

'Is that okay?' says Daniel, feeling bad that Hattie won't get to watch the action.

'Of course,' she says, smiling at him. 'Go on.'

Kissing her, Daniel hurries out of the warmup area and into the rider and owner grandstand to the side of the arena entrance. Doug Wallingford's round has started, and he's approaching the second fence, but his grey horse doesn't look at all settled or happy in his work. A couple of strides out, the horse throws up his head, then plunges forward. He's too deep into the bottom of the fence, and it's only because of the horse's considerable talent that they manage to get over the jump cleanly.

The gelding looks sticky through the treble, his stride is getting shorter and choppier, and his ears are now flat back. As they ride the turn at the end of the arena closest to where Daniel's sitting, he sees that the grey's teeth are bared as he fights Doug's tight hold on the reins. The horse makes an uncomfortable-looking jump over the water tray, then applies the brakes hard as they approach the first of the steeplechase-esque brush fences and skids to a stop in front of it. Doug, not pleased, brings his crop down hard on the horse's quarters.

Daniel winces. The eventers vs show jumpers competition course is meant to be a fusion of fences from both worlds, combining traditional show jumps with some more natural-type fences that you'd find on an eventing cross country course. It's likely the grey gelding has never seen a steeplechase fence before and it's confused him.

Red-faced and clearly furious, Doug brings the horse round for another attempt at the fence. This time, the horse stops several strides out from the jump. Doug kicks him, and when that doesn't work he smacks his crop down onto the horse's rear again. The grey gelding doesn't budge. Doug hits the horse again.

The audience are looking uncomfortable. Some people are shaking their heads, and more than a few have their phones out and are filming. Daniel's not surprised; he hates to see a horse treated that way. Doug's behaviour is getting into misuse of the whip territory.

'And unfortunately that's two refusals and elimination for Doug Wallingford and his own Arthur V,' says the commentator in a tight voice, as the bell rings for a second time to indicate elimination.

Furious, Doug pulls on the reins to turn the grey gelding back towards the arena entrance. But the horse clearly doesn't appreciate the way he's being treated and gives a couple of powerful bucks in protest.

The crowd gasp, and one or two of them clap. Doug is almost unseated, causing him to turn an even deeper shade of puce. Daniel shakes his head. He hates it when riders take out their anger on their horses; it's unforgivable. Hopefully the stewards will speak to Doug about his behaviour. It shouldn't be allowed.

'And last to go in this first round of the eventers vs show jumpers league competition is Fliss Moreton riding her own and her mother's Dark Matter,' says the commentator as Doug leaves the arena and Fliss canters in on her smart black mare. 'This is Fliss's first time competing here at London International Horse Show and she's the youngest rider in this competition.'

'Come on, Fliss,' says Daniel under his breath. 'You've got this.'

She's petrified, he thinks, as a grim-faced Fliss and Dark Matter canter to the first fence and start their round. He watches, hands clasped together, breath held, as the pair have a sticky jump over the first. After that, they seem to grow with confidence over every fence and although they have a pole down over the water tray for four faults, they fly the tricky combination and the final orange bogey fence with style. Fliss is grinning as she rides through the finish, patting Dark Matter's neck over and over again.

Daniel stands up and applauds.

Five minutes later, mounted on The Rogue, Daniel along with the rest of the eventing team are beckoned into the International Arena for the prize-giving. The show jumpers follow them, a respectful distance between the two teams.

The arena has already been cleared of jumps by the ever-efficient ground crew, and two huge flower arrangements have been erected at the far end, between which they've been asked to line up their horses. The band are playing a jazzed-up version of a classical music piece, and the audience are clapping. It's quite something.

'The eventers lead the league competition by six penalties but with three more rounds still to go, there's everything to play for,' says the commentator as the teams reach the far end of the arena and line up for the prize-giving.

That's weird, thinks Daniel, looking along the line and realising the show jumping team is a horse and rider short.

Leaning closer to Greta Wolfe, who is halted beside him, Daniel asks, 'What happened to Doug Wallingford?'

'Word is, the stewards gave him an official reprimand for excessive use of the whip,' says Greta, keeping her voice low. 'Now he is sulking and leaves his teammates to collect his rosette while he shags his head groom in the lorry to console himself.'

Daniel grimaces. 'I'm glad they spoke to him. That sort of behaviour shouldn't be tolerated.'

'Exactly, yes,' says Greta. 'Although I pity his groom. She does like him, apparently, but I doubt his performance is going to be very satisfying for her.'

Daniel nods.

From what he's seen of Doug Wallingford, he doubts it too.

CHAPTER EIGHT

WAYNE

This is the fanciest restaurant Wayne's ever been in. From the classical music playing softly in the background, to the artfully arranged tablescapes and the impeccably turned out, uniformed staff, everything about the place screams exclusivity. He's more of a pub grub, steak-and-ale pie kind of guy, although he's equally happy baking apple crumble or a lasagne to serve himself. Posh restaurants always make him feel as if he's not acting right.

He's wearing a suit too, which is a bit of a first. He'd thought it'd be nice to get dressed up and come to this place but, if he's honest, he's feeling pretty awkward. Still, Megan seems to be enjoying herself, and that's the main thing. Tonight he's got something really special planned. He's nervous, but excited too. He just hopes it all goes to plan.

'This is amazing, isn't it?' says Megan, looking out of the floor-to-ceiling window beside their table. 'It's like we can see the whole world from up here.'

'Totally,' replies Wayne. He can't deny that the view is stunning. Situated on the top floor of one of the tallest buildings in the capital, the restaurant boasts breathtaking panoramic views across the city. After dark, with the lights illuminating the streets and buildings, it really is something. It's breathtaking in other ways too – especially for someone like him who doesn't enjoy heights. He can't deny that the fact they're so far from the ground makes him feel a bit freaked out. Give him the rolling countryside of Leightonshire and his boots firmly on the ground any day.

But he swallows down his fear, and when the waiter comes over to take their order he waits for Megan to say what she'd like first, then goes for the same goat's cheese starter she's having followed by what he hopes is just a fancy version of steak and chips.

When the waiter has gone, Wayne raises his pint to Megan and says, 'Happy Wednesday.'

She laughs, and clinks her wine glass against his pint. 'And to you.' They both take a sip of their drinks, then Megan continues, 'How did today go?'

'Good,' says Wayne, taking another cheeky sip of his beer. 'I was kept pretty busy, all of us farriers were, with loose shoes and horses who'd over-reached and pulled their shoes off. Some bloke from *Horse & House* even came and did an interview with us after lunch. They're doing a "day in the life" series about different jobs at the show, and one of the features is going to be about us farriers.'

'Nice,' says Megan. 'Did you tell them about next year's charity calendar?'

Wayne grins. 'Would've been rude not too.'

The 'Rural Pleasures' charity calendar he'd posed for as 'Mr March' in this year's edition had invited him back to pose for the next one. He did the photoshoot about a month ago, and Megan was on-set (or rather 'in forge') to give him some modelling tips. It had been a real laugh – having Megan there had made things feel less intense than the previous year, and the fact he knew what to expect this time had helped too. Earlier this week, he'd been emailed the image the charity intended to use in the calendar, and he was pleased with how it had turned out. They'd gone for the image of him holding a red-hot iron shoe, straight from the furnace, with only the steam coming off the iron preserving his modesty. Apparently they'd had to add a bit of extra steam digitally in post-production as the original didn't quite cover his essentials. It was, according to Megan's professional eye, super hot.

'If they mention it, I'm sure the charity will get an extra boost in sales,' says Megan, taking another sip of her wine. She gestures towards it. 'This is great.'

'How was your day?' asks Wayne, trying to act like this is just another conversation over dinner like any other day, even though this isn't just any other day. It's a really important, potentially life-changing day. 'You had that campaign shoot, didn't you?'

Megan nods. 'It went well, I think. I mean, I'm still pretty new to it all but the photographer and creative director seemed happy and I thought the pictures looked good.'

'I bet they were stunning,' says Wayne. It's impossible for Megan to take a bad picture. 'What's your next—'

'Excuse me?'

Wayne and Megan turn to see a twentysomething woman with cropped blonde hair wearing a sequined dress hovering nervously beside their table.

The woman clears her throat. She's looking at Megan. 'I just wanted to say I thought what you did a few months ago was incredible. Calling out the haters like that? You're a real inspiration.'

Megan smiles. 'Thank you.'

Wayne has another mouthful of beer and waits while the two women chat for a while, the young woman finally moving away when the starters arrive. It's no big deal. He's got used to people coming up to Megan. Since her Instagram post about knowing your own worth went viral a few months ago, she's amassed a huge following. With the announcement that she's the new face of a major high-end lingerie brand, some stunning photographs from the campaign being featured in the national newspapers, and one being projected onto the front of a couple of iconic London landmarks last week, it's hard for her to go anywhere without being recognised. She handles it with grace, even though she's admitted privately to him that she finds the attention a bit embarrassing.

As they finish eating their starters, Wayne reaches out and takes Megan's hand. 'This is amazing. You're amazing.'

She smiles back at him and squeezes his hand. 'So are you.'

Wayne feels his heart begin to jackhammer in his chest. This is the moment. It's time to do it. Removing his napkin from his lap, he puts it onto the table and stands up. Megan looks confused and he hopes he's not misread the signs – hopes that she wants this as much as he does.

'Megan,' he says, smiling as he gets ready to drop down on one knee. 'I'd—'

'Megan Taylor? Oh my God!' shrieks a loud, fortysomething woman with flame-red hair and wearing an emerald-green shift dress. 'This is so…' The woman turns and waves across to a table of women over on the other side of the restaurant. 'Get over here, quick. It's Megan Taylor.'

Megan looks startled by the woman's enthusiasm. Wayne feels frozen. He doesn't know what to do, but when he sees the red-haired woman's friends getting up from their table and hurrying towards him and Megan, he realises there's no saving this moment.

As Wayne retakes his seat, the women crowd round them. They fangirl over Megan, calling her a role model and applauding her stand against the patriarchy. They ask for autographs, and Megan signs their napkins and train ticket stubs with smiles and thanks. Wayne is proud of her, but he's disappointed too.

After ten minutes, the maître de comes over and asks the

group of ladies to go back to their table. The maître de is extremely apologetic, but it's not his fault. Wayne takes Megan's hand. 'You okay?'

She nods. 'Sorry about that. They were rather… enthusiastic.'

Wayne smiles. 'It's fine. It comes with the territory.'

'I guess,' says Megan – she bites her lip. 'Was there something you were going to say? You know, before they interrupted us?'

He holds her gaze for a moment. Takes her hand in his and replies, 'No, it's all good.'

But it isn't really.

The small box from Tiffany's seems heavier in his suit pocket now. He'd anticipated asking Megan to marry him and hoped, if she said yes, that they'd be drinking celebratory champagne right about now and looking forward to their future together.

But that's not happened. His secret plan has been thwarted, and he realises now that it's going to be a lot more difficult to pull it off than he'd originally realised.

Wayne refuses to be deterred though.

What he needs is a new plan.

THURSDAY

CHAPTER NINE

ELLA

Ella wakes with the worst hangover ever. Her head is pounding. Her body aches. Her tongue feels dry and kind of furry, and there's this awful taste in her mouth. She shudders as she remembers what happened when she was walking the course in the International Arena.

What an idiot.

She's thankful for the pint of water she'd drunk before going to bed, but she still feels really dehydrated. Getting up, she heads to the kitchenette and opens a bottle of water. Downing half of it, she walks through to the tiny bathroom and splashes water on her face.

Staring at herself in the tiny mirror over the mini sink, Ella grimaces. She looks awful – bloodshot eyes, dark circles under them, and her hair is a tangled mess. There's nothing much she can do about the bloodshot eyes, but she slaps on some tinted moisturiser to make herself look a bit less like death warmed up, and runs a brush through her unruly hair. Looking just slightly more in the land of the living, she pulls on her stable gear, then grabs another bottle of water to take with her and heads out of her lorry to the stables.

It's early but the place is already bustling with activity. Competitors and grooms are feeding their horses and sorting out their stables. Some are already out on exercise, using the pre-show familiarisation slots in the International Arena and the London Arena to get their animals acclimatised to their surroundings and give them a loosener. The mix of equines is impressive – there are big competition horses like the show jumpers, eventers and dressage horses, as well as show horses of every size and shape imaginable – from show hacks to mountain and moorland ponies – and then the horses from the King's Troop display team and the racing ponies from the Shetland Pony Grand National.

Eagle's Crest and On-The-Up are awake and looking out over their stable doors. They wicker eagerly when they see her. The grey mare, On-The-Up, bangs the door with a front hoof too – telling Ella she's late with their breakfast.

'Sorry, guys,' says Ella, giving each of the horses a Polo before giving them their feeds and then setting about filling their haynets. 'My bad.'

Once the horses have finished their breakfasts and are munching on their hay, Ella mucks out their stables. She keeps her head down and avoids eye contact with anyone as she wheels her muck barrow along the passageway between the stables to and from the muck trailer. The last thing she wants is for someone to ask her about yesterday's utter disaster.

Once the mucking out is done, she grooms the horses. She's always found grooming therapeutic – the rhythm of brushing is almost like a meditation – and gradually she starts to feel better. With the grooming finished, Ella takes the horses one at a time for a leg stretch in the arena and then re-rugs them. She's just finishing up with Eagle's Crest's rugs when her mobile beeps in her pocket.

She wants to ignore it but she can't. Pulling out her phone, she reads the message on the screen from an unknown number.

Her breath catches in her throat.

DIDN'T SEE YOU ON THE TV LAST NIGHT, WHORE. THE THOUGHT OF ALL THOSE GUYS LAUGHING AT YOU NAKED PUT YOU OFF YOUR GAME? GOOD!!! KEEP IT THAT WAY OR I'LL SEND THEM. HAHAHAHAHAHAHAHA.

Ella stifles a sob. She clenches her fingers tighter around the phone. The message is from Henry again, on yet another number because she blocked the one he used last night. This is impossible. It can't continue. She refuses to let him control her in this way. He can't be allowed to make her feel like shit all the time. And she can't let his threats stop her from competing here.

She takes a deep breath, fighting to control her emotions as the anger, hurt and frustration flood through her.

She *is* going to compete. She can't allow his threats to make her miss her shot at the World Cup Qualifier later this week. She mustn't let him intimidate her.

If he sends the nude pictures to his mates, then so be it – it's a risk she has to take. Although the more she thinks about how possessive and jealous Henry is, the more she doubts that he would actually send the photos to anyone. He's clearly still angry that they broke up, and perhaps in some weird, misguided way he's hopeful they'll get together again. It's never going to happen, though. Literally never. Because it's over between them and his awful behaviour can't continue.

Before she changes her mind, Ella taps out a message:

Henry. Stop this. Harass me again and I'm calling the police. I mean it.

She presses send and waits until the message has been delivered, then she blocks the number and turns off her phone. She's got a bit of time now, so she's going to go out and get herself a new phone and number. Then Henry won't be able to send her messages no matter how many new numbers he gets. The thought makes her feel a bit better. Like she's taking control of the situation.

'How are you doing?' asks a vaguely familiar male voice.

Flinching, Ella spins round and sees Joe Broughton's handsome face looking at her over the top of the stable door. 'Oh, hi. Sorry, I didn't see you there. And I'm okay, thanks.' She shakes her head. 'Well, you know, as okay as I can be with the worst hangover ever.'

Joe grins. 'Ah, yes, sorry about that. I had a feeling you might feel a bit worse for wear this morning.'

'It's not your fault,' says Ella. 'All self-inflicted.'

'Maybe I can help, though,' says Joe. 'Have you eaten breakfast yet? I know a great little café nearby who do the best bacon rolls in London.'

Smiling, Ella cocks her head to the side. 'The best in London, huh? That's quite a claim.'

'Honestly, it's true,' replies Joe.

'Well, okay,' says Ella, her smile broadening. 'Then I think I need to test them out.'

CHAPTER TEN

JOE

'These bacon rolls *are* amazing,' says Ella, after taking her first bite.

'I know, right?' replies Joe. 'Best in London – it says so on the sign.'

Ella follows his gaze to the chalkboard that proudly claims this café makes the best bacon rolls in London, and laughs. 'It does indeed.'

Joe smiles. It's fun hanging out with Ella. Even though he hardly knows her, there's an easy familiarity between them and it feels as if they've been friends forever. She even likes this small no-frills café that's a far cry from the more fancy eateries and pubs that cater for the people going to events at Excel. This place, with its menu written on a wall-mounted whiteboard, its basic décor, wipe-clean red plastic tablecloths, and food dished up in a tiny kitchen and passed through a serving hatch to the lone waitress, is what Joe's dad used to call a greasy spoon – and Joe, like his dad, has always had a soft spot for them.

'Congratulations on the puissance,' says Ella.

'Thanks, I was really pleased with Pipplemouse,' replies Joe. His skewbald gelding jumped tremendously the previous night.

In the puissance, competitors battle it out to jump a wooden wall painted as if it's red brick with white coping stones on the top that increases in height every round. By the time the wall reached 1.75 metres, all the riders were out except for Joe and Doug Wallingford. Doug was riding Paul's Landing, his specialist puissance horse and reigning puissance champion. Joe was riding his skewbald gelding, Pipplemouse. The two of them stayed neck-and-neck until the wall went up to 2.15. Paul's Landing cleared the fence, and Joe's Pipplemouse just touched the white coping stones and one of the lightweight wooden blocks fell. 'It was his first puissance, so to come second was amazing.'

'Cheers to that,' says Ella, picking up her mug of tea and clinking it against Joe's.

Laughing, Joe raises his mug too, and takes a sip. This is nice. Different, but nice. In the past, it would've been him and Dad sitting here this morning, talking about how the classes the previous day had gone. He feels a pang of sadness like a gut-punch to the belly, and quickly looks away and takes another mouthful of tea, trying to hide his suddenly watery eyes from Ella.

It doesn't work, though.

'Are you okay?' she asks, concern on her face.

Joe nods but a muscle pulses in his cheek. 'I was just thinking how pleased Dad would've been.'

'I'm so sorry,' says Ella. She reaches out and pats his arm. 'It must be really tough.'

Joe nods again, unable to trust that his voice won't crack if he replies. His dad, Roger Broughton, had won more World Cups, puissance and Olympic medals than any other British show jumper in history. He'd been one of the most respected people in the business, and after his successful sporting career, he had gone on to a second career presenting equestrian sports on television. When he died suddenly of a heart attack just after coming off air in March, it was a huge shock to everyone. Even now, nine months on, Joe feels his loss as acutely as he did that first day. Dad taught him everything he knows; he'd encouraged his passion for horses and nurtured his talent but never pushed him. He'd been like a Yoda figure and his best mate in one. And now he's gone.

'Your dad was a legend,' says Ella. 'And I bet he'd have been thrilled about your results yesterday.'

'He would've been,' says Joe, emotion making his voice sound thinner. 'And he would've said to let the horse choose his spot to take-off.' Joe gives Ella a rueful smile. 'I told Pipplemouse to get in deep to the wall, but I think he'd have been happier taking off a little further back. Having the brick down was my fault.'

'Then it was a learning experience,' says Ella, gently. 'Next time, you'll know what to do.'

'Very true,' says Joe, smiling wider. He's glad she hasn't asked him if he misses his dad like all the journalists usually do. It's such a stupid and insensitive question – of course he misses him. 'And thanks.'

Ella shrugs. 'For what?'

'For being here.'

'It's my pleasure,' she says, holding up her now-almost-finished bacon roll. 'And I had to test this out, didn't I?'

'True,' he laughs. 'So how did you get into show jumping?'

'Ah, now there's a question,' says Ella, popping the last of her roll into her mouth and making him wait until she's finishing eating before answering. 'I grew up in Birmingham, so I was a real city kid. My mum's a nurse and my dad's an engineer, neither of them had ever ridden a horse, but one Christmas, when I was about nine, my aunt bought me a riding lesson gift voucher for a stables over in Solihull. My mum took me along on a rainy January day and, despite getting drenched riding in the outdoor arena, by the time the forty-five-minute session was over I was totally hooked.'

'So did your parents buy you lessons after that?' asks Joe.

'Occasionally, but they couldn't afford to very often, so I worked as a helper on Saturday and Sunday and in return I'd get one ride per week. It was brilliant. When I was about thirteen, the owner of the stables decided I had some talent and kind of took me under her wing. She had a daughter who was a few years older than me, and when the daughter grew out of her jumping pony, Sparky, they let me have him on loan. He was the most amazing pony. He's what got me into show jumping. Ever since then, it's been my ambition to ride at London International Horse Show.'

'And now you're here,' says Joe. He remembers Ella's incident during the course walk. 'So what happened yesterday?'

She looks down, and for a moment he thinks she's not going to answer.

Ella blows out hard. 'I was an idiot.'

'Did the nerves get to you? It can be really intimidating the first time you—'

'No, it wasn't that,' says Ella, shaking her head. 'It was my ex.'

Joe frowns. 'What did they do?'

Ella holds his gaze, and it feels as if she's weighing up whether to tell him or not. Joe keeps eye contact. He hopes she'll trust him.

'He's been harassing me ever since we broke up,' says Ella, hesitantly. 'Yesterday he sent a message saying unless I withdrew from the show, he'd send naked pictures of me to all his show jumping mates and they'd all be laughing at me in the ring.' She exhales hard. 'Let's just say I didn't handle it well.'

'I'm not surprised,' says Joe, clenching his fists tight around his mug of tea. 'Your ex sounds like a real arsehole. Is he a show jumper? Do I know him?'

'You might,' says Ella quietly. 'He's Henry Pottinger.'

Joe knows all about Henry Pottinger. He grips the mug tighter. 'Yeah, I know him. He was a real dick to my sister Alice a couple of years ago – cheated on her with several other people, then spread a whole load of malicious rumours about her after she'd dumped him.'

'I'm sorry she had to go through that,' says Ella. 'He cheated on me too. That's why I dumped him.'

Joe shakes his head. 'I'm sorry he's behaving so badly towards you. I guess he's still pulling the same old shit. If I can help in any way just—'

'Thanks, but I'm going to change my number so hopefully that'll stop him. If not, I've told him I'll report his behaviour to the police.'

'Good plan,' says Joe. 'You're well out of that relationship.'

He can't believe bloody Henry Pottinger is still pulling the crap he pulled with Alice. Even though they'd come up the show jumping ranks on ponies together, Joe had never been mates with him. Always charming in a rather arrogant, brash way, Henry was never short of friends or horses, but there's something about the guy – a mean streak – that Joe never liked or trusted, even before Henry did the dirty on his sister.

Someone needs to teach him some manners.

CHAPTER ELEVEN

WAYNE

The alarm clock beeps Wayne awake. It's almost nine-thirty – far later than he'd ever get up normally – but as he's working the late shift today he doesn't have to rush. Turning off the alarm, he stretches and turns over. Beside him, Megan is still snoozing peacefully, seemingly oblivious to the alarm. Even in her sleep, she looks as gorgeous as ever.

He smiles. It's not often they get to enjoy a lie-in so this feels like a real luxury. He snuggles into Megan and kisses her forehead. Last night, his plan to propose was scuppered, but he refuses to let it ruin this for him. He's going to make another plan, find a better place to propose, and make it happen. This setback isn't going to deter him.

Wayne's stomach rumbles. It sounds like a thunderclap to him, but Megan doesn't seem to have noticed. Relieved, he nestles closer to her.

His stomach growls. Louder this time, and he feels the hunger pangs. Megan's eyelids flicker and she murmurs something he can't make out, but doesn't wake. It's a close one, though.

Sitting up, Wayne swings his legs over the side of the king-size bed and stands. The room is almost as big as the entire ground floor of his small terraced cottage back home and no way near as chaotic. Here, it's all off-whites and beiges from the wall paint to the sofa and cushions, the bedding and the floor-to-ceiling curtains that are currently obscuring the view over the river. It's nice, but a bit bland for Wayne's tastes.

His stomach roars again, and he pads over to the desk and the room service menu sitting on it. Keeping his voice low, he dials the number on the phone and orders – full English for them both, toast, some pastries and a fruit plate.

With Megan still snoozing, Wayne busies himself making them coffee at the in-room coffee station – an alcove fitted out with a fancy coffee-maker and a huge selection of different coffees with strengths from weak to nuclear. He goes for a mid-range blend and fills the machine with water once he's found the place it's meant to go – which wasn't super easy.

'Too fancy for your own good,' Wayne mutters under his breath as he switches on the machine. He prefers a kettle and some instant every day of the week – much less hassle.

With the coffee done, Wayne's just carrying it over to the bed when there's a knock on the door. Putting both mugs down on his bedside table, he heads back across the room to the door.

'Hi,' he says.

If the room service lady in her smart navy uniform is surprised by him opening the door in his boxers, she doesn't show it. 'Good morning, sir.' She gestures towards the two silver trays on her trolley. 'Where would you like this?'

'Just in here on the desk would be great,' Waynes says, stepping aside to let her in.

He waits by the door while she unloads the trays and then wheels her trolley back out to the corridor.

'Sign here, please,' she says, holding out a handheld device for him to autograph with his finger.

He does as she asks, thanks her and then closes the door.

One by one, Wayne removes the silver domes covering the

food. It smells amazing and his stomach is rumbling again, this time in anticipation.

'That smells good,' says Megan, blinking as she opens her eyes.

'I wasn't sure what you'd want so I ordered pretty much everything,' says Wayne. 'What can I get you?'

Megan scans the food spread out across the desk. 'I'll start with the full English please.'

'Coming up, m'lady,' says Wayne, grinning as he picks up one of the plates and takes it across to Megan. 'Your wish is my command.'

Megan laughs. 'You know this could be a new career for you if you ever get bored of being a farrier.'

'What could?' asks Wayne.

'The semi-naked butler thing,' says Megan, smiling. 'You look hot.'

'For your eyes only,' says Wayne, grabbing his plate of full English from the desk and going back over to join Megan in the bed. 'I don't serve breakfast in bed to just anyone, you know.'

'I'm glad to hear it.' She takes a mouthful of scrambled eggs and sausage. 'Oh my God, this is amazing.'

She's not wrong. The food tastes great. They work their way through the full English, the toast and most of the fruit plate. Afterwards, they're so stuffed, they sit on the bed chatting for nearly an hour before either of them feel able to move.

'I'd better get in the shower,' says Wayne, after checking the time on his watch. 'I need to start my shift in just over an hour.'

'Okay, cool,' replies Megan. 'I'll walk over to Excel with you. Daniel's jumping again this afternoon so I'd like to be there to support him and Hattie.'

'Great idea,' says Wayne, leaning over and kissing Megan before getting up.

Leaving Megan in bed, he walks across the room to the ensuite. It's far bigger than his cottage's little bathroom. To be honest, the huge shower alone is bigger. Slipping off his boxers, he turns on the shower and then steps inside, closing his eyes as the water cascading from the two rainfall shower heads and numerous body jets flows over him.

He doesn't hear Megan join him, but he feels her hands as they slide down his chest, and her lips as she kisses him. Opening his eyes, Wayne sees her standing in front of him. Her long hair is already slicked back from the water and in her eyes is the look he's come to know so very well.

As he rises to attention, Megan takes him in her hand and he groans. Pulling her to him, he kisses her hard, running his hands over her body, feeling every curve and dip. Wanting her. From the urgency of her kisses, he knows she feels the same way.

Wayne groans again. It's all he can do not to cum right now.

She's so sexy.

With Megan's back against the shower wall, Wayne lifts her up so she's astride him and enters her in one smooth thrust. She feels amazing, and as he plunges into her, she grips his buttocks, pulling him deeper. Wanting him.

'Fuck me, Wayne,' she whispers in his ear. 'Harder.'

He does as she commands. The water pours over them, the steam swirls around them and the sensations heighten. It's hot in every way.

I'm the luckiest man alive.

CHAPTER TWELVE

HATTIE

'You made it,' says Hattie, as she waves at Lady Pat, who's wearing her usual Barbour jacket over a purple trouser suit, and her ever-loyal personal assistant alongside her, Gerald Talbot – an impeccably dressed, tweed jacket-wearing sixty-something man with an unrivalled air of quiet efficiency about him.

'Of course, dear,' replies Lady Pat, waiting as Gerald shows their passes to the security crew at the entrance to the stables. 'I wouldn't have missed this for the world, and Gerald has always been rather keen on this show.'

Hattie's surprised; she never realised Gerald even liked horses. 'Is that right?'

Gerald's usually stiff-upper-lip unflappable demeanour changes, his cheeks turning pink as he nods. 'Well, like everyone, I do enjoy watching the Shetland Pony Grand National and the dog agility championship. And, of course, the Christmas Finale with the snow and Father Christmas is always rather charming.'

'Of course,' says Hattie, glancing at Lady Pat. 'The Christmas Finale is the best bit.'

'Absolutely,' says Lady Pat, giving Hattie a wink. 'Now, where's Daniel and how is it all going?'

'He's in the warmup,' says Hattie. 'Come, it's this way.'

She leads Lady Pat and Gerald through the Hand & Flower beer garden and round to the champagne viewing lawn, which they have passes for, then on into the collecting ring where the riders are warming up for the next round of the eventers vs show jumpers league competition. Although the afternoon performance started almost an hour ago, there's still a lot of people gathered around the collecting ring rather than in their seats in the international arena.

Daniel is riding Pink Fizz in the competition today, the gelding's distinctive pink roan colour making him easy to spot amongst the bays, greys and chestnuts all getting ready for the next class. Finding a spot to watch, Hattie leans on the fence, as does Gerald, while Lady Pat unfolds her shooting stick and takes a seat.

They watch as Greta takes a flyer over the practice fence on Westworlder, with the gelding letting rip a noisy fart as he lands, causing Greta to laugh out loud. Fergus Bingley pops the jump a few moments later on Dodger in his usual foot-perfect fashion. Antonio de Luca, who'll be the first to jump for the show jumpers, is having his horse's boots checked by his groom, and Doug Wallingford is cantering around on his rather unhappy-looking grey horse Arthur V. As the horse goes past them, Hattie winces as she sees the whites of the horse's eyes as he throws up his head and fights at Doug's strong rein contact. To Hattie, it's as if she can feel the horse's discomfort in her own body.

'Afternoon, Lady P,' says Daniel, riding over to them on a bouncy-looking Pink Fizz. 'Good to see you, Gerald.'

'How's he settling?' asks Lady Pat, gesturing towards the roan gelding. 'You don't think the atmosphere might be a bit much for him?'

Pink Fizz is a real livewire – super talented but quirky and prone to acting out if he gets too tense or the situation is too buzzed. Hattie had some reservations about Daniel bringing him, given he's not always the most reliable, but Daniel felt the experience would be useful to the gelding.

'He's good,' says Daniel, stroking the horse's neck. 'He's handled everything like a pro so far, and we've stuffed his ear cover with cotton wool to muffle the sounds of the audience when we're in the arena.'

'Excellent,' replies Lady Pat, nodding approvingly. 'And your team mates, how are they doing?'

'They're all on form,' says Daniel. 'It's been a bit of an eye-opener for Fliss but she did a great job yesterday.'

'She did,' says Gerald. 'We were cheering you all on when they showed the highlights on telly last night.'

'It was good to see the eventers take an early lead,' says Lady Pat, nodding. 'Now you just need to—'

She's interrupted by a loud crash from one of the practice fences as Doug Wallingford's grey gelding crashes through a tall upright fence, scattering the blue-and-orange poles.

'Bloody animal,' says Doug, cursing. 'Do as you're told.'

The gelding doesn't want to, though. Throwing up his head, he tries to evade Doug's attempts to turn him. Finding the reins too restrictive, the horse twists his head and then plunges forwards, humping his back and putting in a succession of large bucks.

Taken by surprise, Doug is almost dislodged from the saddle. This seems to make him more angry and he gives the gelding a sharp kick and a whack with his crop. The horse hurtles forwards, still fighting for his head. Doug, muttering under his breath, wrestles the gelding back under control.

Hattie can hardly bear to watch.

Keeping the gelding in canter, Doug rides him towards the second practice fence – a large oxer of orange-and-blue poles. The horse looks as if he's taking it on but then, at the last possible moment, he slams on the brakes. Doug realises too late, and as the grey gelding lowers his head, Doug flies out the front door and into the poles with another almighty clatter.

Free from restriction, the horse spins round and bolts across the warmup area, almost jumping the white railings into the viewing area before thinking twice at the last moment and swerving sharply. He gallops, hurtling around the warmup. Wide eyed and panicked.

The security guys on the gate close it to prevent the gelding running back to the stables. The other competitors react just as quickly, asking their horses to stop and stand still. The horse weaves between them for a few laps of the warmup, then comes to an abrupt halt in the corner furthest away from the practice fences, not far from where they are.

Seeing that Doug's still on the floor by the jump and that his groom is with him, Hattie ducks under the railings and moves calmly towards the big grey.

'Hey, boy, it's okay,' she says, her tone gentle.

The horse snorts, his head high as he looks at her with distrusting eyes.

'You're okay,' Hattie says. She keeps her breathing slow and steady. 'But you can't stay loose, can you?'

He's still eying her suspiciously, but he allows her to move closer.

'There you go,' says Hattie, calmly taking another couple of steps towards him. 'Clever boy.'

She's close now, really close, but as she moves to take his reins, Arthur V steps back a couple of paces. Hattie sees that he's shaking.

She pauses where she is and takes a deep breath in and then a long, loud breath out. The horse, who seems to be holding his breath, watches her for a moment then blows out and lowers his head a fraction.

'Good boy,' says Hattie. 'Don't worry, I'm not going to hurt you.'

The horse takes another deeper breath. This time when Hattie steps forward, he allows her to take hold of his reins.

'There you go, that wasn't so bad, was it?' she says, stroking the horse's dappled, sweat-drenched neck as the other riders start to continue with their warmup routines.

They stand together for a few minutes until Arthur V stops shaking and the wild look is gone from his eyes. Hattie strokes his forehead and he lowers his head more, a sure sign that he's starting to relax.

'There you go,' says Hattie, smiling as the horse nestles his head against her. 'What a sweet boy you are.'

'Come here, you bloody animal,' says an angry male voice behind them.

The horse flinches, and throws his head up.

Hattie turns to see Doug Wallingford storming across the warmup towards them. He's a big guy – six foot three, or maybe six foot four, and he towers over Hattie as he snatches the grey's reins from her. 'Thanks for catching it. Bloody thing, trying to make a fool of me.'

'I don't think he was trying to do anything,' says Hattie, as diplomatically as she can, although what she really wants to do is tell Doug he's treating the horse all wrong. 'He's just sensitive.'

'What are you, some kind of horse shrink?' scoffs Doug, looking her up and down. 'This horse is a pain in my arse. Too up itself by far.'

The implication in his stare is that Hattie is the same.

To hell with diplomacy.

'Maybe if you treated him better, he'd want to jump for you,' she retorts, standing her ground. 'Haven't you already had a warning for overuse of the whip?'

'Fuck off,' growls Doug, yanking Arthur V's reins and forcing the horse to follow him back across the arena.

Hattie feels tears prick at her eyes as she watches the gelding being dragged away by Doug. It feels as if a knife is twisting in her heart. She might have only just met the horse but he reminds her so strongly of Mermaid's Gold on the day that she arrived – all that fear and distrust of humans, but the willingness to forgive too.

Maybe that's why she feels such a strong connection to him.

CHAPTER THIRTEEN

DANIEL

With Pink Fizz loosened up, Daniel dismounts and Hattie throws the roan gelding's Thermatex rug over the horse and saddle to keep him warm until it's time for him and Daniel to do their final preparations for jumping. Lady Pat and Gerald have gone to find their seats in the stands – keen to watch all the competitors jumping in this round of the eventers vs show jumpers league competition.

'You okay?' asks Daniel, as Hattie finishes buckling Pink Fizz's underbelly strap.

'Yeah,' says Hattie, but her voice sounds flat and she's frowning.

Daniel raises an eyebrow. 'Really? I can tell something's bothering you.'

'Sorry, it's okay, though. You need to be focusing on the competition.'

'I'm last to jump. I've got a while before I need to get my game face on.'

Hattie smiles. 'Okay, then, it's about Doug Wallingford and his grey horse, Arthur V. I can't get how he treated him out of my mind. That poor horse.'

Of course.

'It wasn't good,' agrees Daniel.

'It really wasn't, and Doug was so angry. I just hate how he treated that poor boy.'

Daniel nods. 'I heard from Greta that Doug's wife threw him out a month or so ago and he only has very limited access to see the kids. If he's stressed about that, maybe it's carrying over to how he is with his horses?'

'If he acted the way he did with me towards her, I'm not surprised she kicked him out,' says Hattie. 'He's holding so much anger, but he shouldn't be taking it out on the horse.'

'Very true.' Daniel hadn't met Doug before this week, so he has no idea how the man usually behaves, but he wasn't impressed by what he saw today. 'Maybe it's best to stay out of his way?'

'I don't know if I can. That poor horse was so afraid. He can't stay with that awful man; it would break him and my heart.' Hattie sighs. 'I feel like I have to do something.'

Daniel holds her gaze for a long moment. He loves how passionate Hattie is about horses and their welfare, and how she can't walk away from an animal in need. He puts his arms around her, pulling her into a hug. 'I'd expect no less.'

~

It's down to the last rider from each team to jump, and the score in this round of the eventers vs show jumpers competition is currently a tie. The course has been causing its fair share of trouble, with a treble of maximum height verticals built with white poles being the main culprit.

For the eventers, Fliss Moreton had a great clear round, as did Jonathan Scott, then Fergus Bingley had an unlucky pole down at the last element of the treble, when Dodger got in a bit too deep after making up ground through the first elements, and Greta Wolfe had the middle and last elements down.

On the show jumpers' side, Antonio de Luca jumped a great clear, and Fernando Alma, Clara Philips, Emma Holmer-Watson and Joe Broughton have each had a fence down. Daniel and Doug Wallingford are the last to jump.

As Daniel rides into the arena on Pink Fizz, he feels the roan gelding's stride falter. The horse has never been in an environment like this, and it's clear that the party atmosphere is having an effect. Daniel just hopes that he's right about the horse and that he'll enjoy it.

Keeping the gelding in walk for as long as he can to give him time to have a look at what's going on – the electronic advertising boards that line the outside of the arena, the brightly lit course of show jumps and, of course, the huge crowd gathered in the grandstands – Daniel waits until it's almost thirty seconds since the buzzer has sounded before asking Pink Fizz to canter and heading down towards the first fence. He knows he's cutting it close to the 45-second time limit to begin jumping the course once the judges have given the signal to start, but every second counts towards helping this less-experienced horse settle into his environment.

It seems to work. Pink Fizz pops easily over the first fence and is settled and focused on the job as they spring over the planks at two, and a large spread with dancing snowmen painted onto the filler at three. They make the turn into the water tray smoothly and fly over that and the oxer double that comes after it before looping back to a brush fence and fake stone wall on a dog-leg turn.

But that's where things start to go wrong. As they land over the fake stone wall, the flashes of several cameras go off directly in the stands ahead of them. Pink Fizz snorts, spooking sideways away from the sudden light.

'Steady,' says Daniel, trying to calm the gelding, but the horse accelerates, his concentration broken.

There's a loud inhale from the audience.

The next fence is a maximum-height triple bar. Pink Fizz sees the fence but he's travelling too fast and too flat, and it's only because of the horse's immense talent that he manages to clear it.

Daniel touches the horse's neck. 'Good boy, steady.'

Pink Fizz gives a little curl of his head, as if to say he's okay, but to Daniel the horse doesn't feel as focused or balanced as before as they make the turn towards the troublesome triple of white fences. He asks the gelding for a half-halt to steady him, and the horse responds well, too well, causing them to lose much of their forward momentum.

Shit.

Daniel sees a stride but they're now low on impulsion with a lot of ground to make up. He urges Pink Fizz on, and the gelding does a valiant job of getting to a good spot for take-off, but he's still a bit far off. He leaps and almost clears the first element, but rubs the top pole with his toe, causing it to fall.

The crowd in the grandstands gasps.

But Pink Fizz is a professional. He makes up the ground between the first and second elements and jumps cleanly over the second and third element to finish the course with just one fence down.

Delighted, Daniel rubs the horse's neck. 'Good boy, that was great.'

As they leave the arena, the commentator reminds the audience that no flash photography is permitted during the competition, then introduces Doug Wallingford riding B&F Electrical's Bright Spark III.

Interesting, thinks Daniel, riding through the archway into the collecting ring. Doug's swapped onto a different horse since the incident with Arthur V.

'Well done, that was amazing, he did so well,' says Hattie,

rushing up to Daniel. 'He tried so hard for you and recovered fast after those idiots spooked him.'

'I know, wasn't he great?' replies Daniel, patting the roan gelding's neck again. 'That fence down was my mistake. He was a star.'

'He was.' Hattie grins, feeding Pink Fizz a Polo from her pocket and then throwing the Thermatex over his quarters to keep him warm until the prize-giving. 'Did you see that Doug's switched horses?'

Daniel nods. 'Yeah.'

'Probably for the best,' says Hattie. 'After the state he whipped poor Arthur V into.'

'Have you thought any more about that?' asks Daniel.

'Yes,' says Hattie. 'But I haven't made a firm decision yet. I think I might—'

She's interrupted by the loudspeaker they're standing beside spluttering into life, and the commentator's plummy voice announcing, 'And that's a clear round for Doug Wallingford and Bright Spark III, which puts the show jumpers ahead of the eventers in today's competition and gives them one win apiece in the league so far.'

~

'There's no justice,' says Hattie, watching as Doug dismounts from Bright Spark III after the prize-giving without even giving the horse a pat. 'Although for his horse's sake, I'm pleased; maybe he won't be so hateful if he's doing well.'

'Maybe,' says Daniel, although he has his doubts. Doug seems so amped up that the slightest thing could set him off.

Getting off Pink Fizz, Daniel runs up his stirrups and loosens the gelding's girth before stepping aside to let Hattie throw a rug over the horse.

Hattie glances back towards Doug. 'Are you okay here for a minute?'

'Sure,' says Daniel, fastening the front strap of the rug.

'Thanks.' Hattie turns across the collecting ring, hurrying towards where Doug is standing chatting to his teammate Antonio.

Doug frowns as he sees her approaching, and Hattie hasn't even spoken to him before a look of fury creases the man's face.

Daniel reads Doug's lips as he spits, 'Piss off, will you.'

He watches as the show jumper makes a dismissive hand gesture, waving Hattie away like she's an annoying bug. Beside him, Antonio looks shocked.

'Pathetic,' says Hattie, shaking her head as she turns away from the show jumpers.

She walks back to Daniel. 'He won't even speak to me.'

Daniel clenches his fists as he fights the urge to go over to Doug and ask him what his problem is. He knows Hattie wouldn't thank him for jumping in; she's more than capable of fighting her own battles.

Still, it really pisses him off to see the show jumper treat Hattie so dismissively, and he can only imagine it's made Hattie even more determined to get Arthur V, the grey gelding, away from Doug.

The question is: how?

CHAPTER FOURTEEN

ELLA

This time, Ella walks the course sober.

This evening, she's competing in the Christmas Bauble Speed Stakes, and she's nervous. In the competition, the horses and their riders compete in heats of two – racing over identical courses that mirror each other on either side of the arena. It's fast and adrenaline-fuelled, and she's never done a class like it before.

Butterflies flutter in her belly as she makes her way through the entrance to the international arena and across the synthetic sand to the start of the course, making sure to give the flower-and-fountain ornamental display she passes a wide berth, just in case. She doesn't want a repeat of yesterday's embarrassment.

'Ella? Wait up.'

She turns to see Joe hurrying to catch up with her. Smiling, she waits for him to reach her. 'Hi.'

'How's it going?' asks Joe.

'I'm sober, if that's what you mean.'

Joe looks mortified. 'I wasn't asking—'

'I know,' says Ella, laughing as she gives him a light punch on the arm. 'I'm okay, thanks. A bit nervous, but otherwise good.'

'No more hassle from your ex?' says Joe, as they walk around the first fence – an inviting black-and-white oxer – and on to the second.

'Thankfully no,' says Ella. 'I've got a new phone number now, so hopefully he won't be able to contact me again.'

'Great,' says Joe. 'That's really good news.'

They walk around fence two – a tall blue gate with fake snow on the top – and stop, considering the turn to fence three, a maximum-height vertical of planks. There are two ways you could play it – the safe way is to go around the outside of the strategically placed flower arrangement, but that will take up a lot of time, or there's the faster but more risky route of cutting inside the flower arrangement and taking the jump on an angle.

'Thoughts?' asks Joe, looking at Ella.

She mimes zipping her lips. 'It's a race. I'm not telling you my secrets.'

Joe laughs. 'Fair enough.'

They walk on in a companionable silence, past the planks and through a dog-leg turn to a double of oxers sporting some brightly painted 'elf' fillers. Ella glances at Joe as he strides out the double – measuring the distance so he knows whether his horse will need to take a big stride or a shorter stride in order to get the best jump over the second part of the double. He's nothing like she'd thought he'd be. Even though he's pretty much from a family that's show jumping royalty, he's kind and funny and seems to like hanging out with an unknown rider like her.

Noticing her watching him, Joe raises an eyebrow. 'You okay?'

'I'm good,' she says. 'Just seeing if I can work out your strategy.'

'Never,' says Joe, laughing as they follow the course, looping back around to a treble of red-and-gold poles with Christmas cracker fillers, and on to the final fence with huge red Christmas baubles and a gold pole.

As they reach the finish line, Ella stops and looks back,

mentally jumping her route through the fences. When she's finished, she looks at Joe. 'What do you think of the course?'

'Well, I'm not going to share my secrets…' He smirks. 'But I think it's a fair test. That turn from two to three is probably going to be the most influential.'

~

Joe's right. The turn between fences two and three proves to be the most influential spot on the course. Ella feels lucky that On-The-Up is such a clean, careful jumper – they win their first two rounds and now they're into the semi-final.

Her heart races as they ride into the arena. On-The-Up jigs, excited to be back in the spotlight, and Ella smiles. The grey mare has always loved an audience, and this evening she's got her biggest one yet – every seat in the international arena is filled. Ella has never had so many people watching her ride, and that's not even including the people tuning in to the equestrian streaming channel or the highlights show on the telly.

She takes a breath, trying to steady her nerves, and puts all thoughts of people watching her from her mind.

The starter beckons her and Doug Wallingford, who's riding his bay gelding Spicetown, over to the start line. As they try to keep their horses still – something that has got much harder after the first round as they're anticipating what's coming next – the starter raises his red flag.

'Are you ready?' asks the starter, smartly dressed in a dark blue suit.

Both Ella and Doug nod.

'Okay, three, two, one… go!' says the starter.

Ella gives On-The-Up the signal and they leap into action. Focused only on her own round, Ella pilots the horse over the first two fences and then takes the tighter turn to three and pushes on through the dog leg. On-The-Up feels like she's loving every moment of it, and as they jump through the treble and hurry towards the last fence Ella can hear the crowd shouting their names.

'Come on, Ella.'

'Go, go, go, On-The-Up.'

'Faster, faster, Ella.'

Crouched low over the mare's neck, Ella's never jumped fences this high at this kind of speed before. It's exhilarating. Liberating, even. And as On-The-Up flies over the final fence and the crowd cheers, Ella thinks it's the best moment of her life.

'Good girl, clever girl,' says Ella, patting On-The-Up's neck again and again.

As she brings the horse back to a walk, Ella glances up at the clock displaying her and Doug's times side-by-side.

They're not fast enough to win.

'And that was a really close one,' says the plummy-sounding commentator. 'Doug Wallingford with Spicetown and Ella Cooper with On-The-Up both go fast and clear, with just six-tenths of a second between them, but the semi-final goes to Doug Wallingford, so he'll be going through into the final with Joe Broughton in just a few minutes.'

'Well done,' says Ella to Doug, as they head back out through the exit into the collecting ring.

'Cheers,' says Doug, hardly looking at her.

Refusing to let his rather dismissive treatment of her impact how she's feeling, Ella dismounts On-The-Up, runs up her stirrups and loosens the horse's girth. Feeding the mare one of her favourite herbal treats, Ella leads her over to where she left her show rug draped over the railings.

'Bad luck,' says Joe, riding over on his pretty chestnut mare, MXA Royal Lion. 'Holly says you jumped a superb round.'

Holly, Joe's head groom, is walking behind Lion, carrying a rug and grooming kit. She smiles. 'I was rooting for you. It was so close, and I really thought you had it. Well done for a cracking round.'

'Thank you,' Ella says to them both. She looks up at Joe. 'Good luck in the final. I've got everything crossed for you.'

'Thanks,' says Joe, grinning. 'See you on the other side.'

As he rides off towards the entrance to the arena, Ella turns back to On-The-Up and feeds her another herbal treat. The mare munches it quickly, then nudges Ella's hand for a third.

Ella laughs. 'More?'

She takes a fourth treat from her pocket and gives it to the mare, who takes it eagerly. 'That's all I've got, though. You'll have to wait until we're back at the stables for more.'

'If you want to watch Joe, I can hold her for a few minutes if you like?' says Holly.

'Are you sure?' asks Ella. 'You don't want to watch?'

'I've seen him jump a million times, I can miss it this once,' says Holly. 'Really, I'd be happy to.'

Throwing her rug over On-The-Up's back, Ella smiles as she hands the mare's reins to Holly. 'Thank you.'

'It's no problem,' says Holly. 'Go on, or you'll miss it.'

Racing out of the collecting ring and into the riders, friends and family section of the grandstand, Ella makes it to a seat just in time. Doug Wallingford and his bay gelding, Spicetown, are riding the left-hand side course, and Joe and his feisty chestnut mare, MXA Royal Lion, are riding on the right.

The audience hushes as the pairs of horse and rider go under starter's orders, then the starter drops the red flag and they're off.

Doug and Spicetown are fastest over the first fence, but Joe and MXA Royal Lion aren't far behind him.

Doug is riding aggressively from the off, kicking the big bay gelding with his spurs, trying to get every ounce of speed from him, whereas Joe sits lightly on his horse and looks as if he's barely doing anything.

As they hurtle over fence two, Joe's horse looks like she's receiving instructions from her rider telepathically, making the tight turn back to three look easy. Doug, on the other hand, pulls hard on his inside rein, bending Spicetown's neck round too far too fast and the horse stumbles.

The crowd gasp.

Doug kicks on, and Spicetown somehow manages to keep going and clear the planks. The crowd cheers and the riders race on, through the dog-leg turn and the 'elf' oxers, then looping back around to a treble of red-and-gold poles with Christmas cracker fillers. They're neck and neck as they approach the treble, but MXA Royal Lion isn't on a good stride and Joe takes a light check on the rein to adjust their position, letting Doug surge ahead.

Inwardly, Ella groans.

Come on, Joe.

Both horses jump through the treble well, but Doug is maintaining his lead. The crowd have started to cheer them on as the riders make the turn to the final fence with huge red Christmas baubles underneath and a gold pole.

Doug's still ahead. Ella clenches her fingers tight.

The audience's cheers and their shouts of encouragement crescendo.

'Come on, Joe,' yells Ella as the adrenaline pumps through her. 'Come on, Lion.'

They're almost at the last fence. Doug is pushing Spicetown to maximum speed, whereas Joe is riding as quietly and calmly as always. Reaching the fence, both horses take off, with Spicetown just half a head in front of MXA Royal Lion, and fly. But as they land, there's a groan from some of the audience.

What's happened?

Then she sees it – Spicetown has knocked the top pole down.

Joe and MXA Royal Lion are clear. Joe is the winner.

Ella leaps to her feet, cheering and clapping.

She's so happy for Joe, it almost feels as if she's won the class herself.

CHAPTER FIFTEEN

DANIEL

The champagne bar is crammed with people and Daniel is relieved to see that Lady Pat and Gerald have managed to get a table.

'There they are,' says Hattie, pointing across the space.

'Great,' replies Daniel, taking Hattie's hand as they head towards their friends.

It's slow going. Now that the last jumping class of the evening is finished, a lot of the show jumpers and their sponsors and friends are here, celebrating or commiserating what the day and evening have brought.

The bar has a good view of the collecting ring, and there are still people and horses milling around inside. The last act – a daring Flying Horsemen display set to music – is taking place in the international arena at the moment, and the performers who will enact the daily Christmas Finale, complete with Santa in his sleigh pulled by two white ponies, are getting warmed up.

Here in the bar, Christmas music is playing over the sound system, and Daniel and Hattie weave their way through the packed bar area in time to 'Merry Christmas Everyone' by Shakin' Stevens.

They wave hello to Greta and Helga, who are speaking German with the group of people they're having a drink with, and continue on towards their friends. Lady Pat and Gerald's table is over on the far side of the bar area, sandwiched between a group of riders still in their breeches and boots, and a table of fortysomething ladies wearing full length evening dress who, from the number of empty champagne bottles and the raucous laughter, look to be having a great night.

'Help yourself,' says Lady Pat, pushing the open bottle of champagne nestled in a silver ice bucket towards them as Daniel and Hattie take a seat at the table.

They sink down onto the seats opposite Lady Pat and Gerald. As Daniel undoes his stock and puts it in the pocket of his jacket, Hattie takes two spare glasses and pours the champagne, passing one to him.

'Thanks,' says Daniel. He raises his glass and looks from Hattie to Lady Pat and Gerald. 'Cheers, everyone. Thanks so much for being here and supporting me.'

Lady Pat smiles. 'Cheers to you, Daniel. Just make sure you beat those show jumpers, yes?'

'I'll do my best.' Daniel takes a sip of the champagne. He hasn't eaten much today and it immediately feels as if the alcohol has gone to his head. He could do with some crisps to go with it, but the queue for the bar is longer than ever so he stays put.

'You and the show jumpers are tied at the moment with a win each,' says Gerald, looking earnest. 'As there's three more rounds of the competition to go, you need to win at least two.'

'Exactly,' says Lady Pat. 'And those show jumpers will certainly give you a run for your money. They're on home turf, so to speak, whereas you lot are the interlopers.'

'It's true,' says Daniel, nodding. 'But I'm pleased with how The Rogue and Pink Fizz are handling the change in environment. Hopefully us eventers will be able to pull it out of the bag.'

'Precisely. On balance, I felt your team did a better job, even if you lost the round,' says Lady Pat, removing a small leather-bound notebook from her pocket. 'I took a few notes on form and the like, which might be useful?'

'Absolutely,' says Daniel, leaning closer. It's always interesting to hear Lady Pat's ideas. She's very astute; nothing much gets past her.

As they debrief on how each competitor jumped in the eventers vs show jumpers competition, Daniel notices that Hattie is unusually quiet. Putting his hand on hers, he asks, 'You okay?'

'Yeah,' says Hattie, but she doesn't look it; her pensive expression is at odds with her reply.

'You sure?' says Daniel. He thinks for a moment. Hattie is one of the most positive and happy people he knows. If she's quiet, it's usually because she's concerned about something, and that something is usually an animal. 'Are you worrying about the grey horse, Arthur V?'

Hattie gives him a sad smile. 'I am.'

'What's this?' asks Lady Pat.

Hattie looks across the table at Lady Pat and Gerald, who are both watching her with concern. 'I'm okay, it's just that I can't get what happened in the warmup earlier with that grey gelding and Doug Wallingford out of my mind. I tried to talk to Doug after the eventers vs show jumpers competition had finished, but he wasn't interested.' She shakes her head. 'There's something about that horse that made me feel instantly connected to him. I feel like I have to do something.'

'Of course, you must do something,' says Lady Pat, in her usual no-nonsense way. 'Don't be deterred just because that show jumping fellow gave you the brush off. If it's important, then you have to try again.'

Hattie nods. 'You're right. I will.'

'Good,' says Lady Pat.

As Hattie, Lady Pat and Gerald talk strategies for getting Doug Wallingford to be more receptive, Daniel takes another sip of his champagne. It's nice to have a bit of downtime. It's been hectic ever since they arrived here at the show. They've got their routine for staying overnight at horse trials well established, but staying here, at an indoor show, seems very different. He can't deny the whole thing is run very efficiently, but without the rolling countryside around him, it feels a little bit like living in a pressure cooker to Daniel.

He takes another sip of champagne, then suddenly shivers. It feels as if someone just walked over his grave.

Putting his glass down, he looks round. He has the weirdest feeling that someone's watching him.

Daniel scans the bar. 'Fairytale of New York' by The Pogues and Kirsty MacColl is playing over the sound system, and everyone here looks like they're having a great time, from the fortysomething ladies playing some kind of drinking game, to the riders chilling out after the day of competition, and on the further tables the couples and groups of spectators, some with a mountain of shopping bags around their feet. Every one of them has their attention on their companions rather than him. He can't see anyone watching him.

Still rather unnerved, Daniel turns back around.

Almost immediately, he shivers again. The hairs on the back of his neck stand up. There's a prickling sensation across his skin.

The sensation of being watched is stronger this time.

Glancing over his shoulder again, he scans the bar area, but still none of the people here are looking in his direction. It's so weird, but even when he turns back around, the unpleasant sensation remains.

It's so weird. I don't like it.

As 'Fairytale of New York' fades and 'Last Christmas' by Wham! begins, he rejoins the conversation with Hattie, Lady Pat and Gerald. But no matter how hard he tries, Daniel can't shake the feeling that something bad is going to happen.

CHAPTER SIXTEEN

JOE

This late in the evening, it's all quiet in the stables. The only sounds are the rhythmic munching of the horses and the occasional noise of a door bolt being slid into place as late-night checks are completed. Most riders let their grooms do the last checks, but Joe has always loved doing his own. He loves the peace of this time of the day, when the classes have finished and most people are back in their lorries or hotels. Hanging out with the horses is the best way he's found to relax.

He lets himself into Royal Lion's stable. The chestnut has a sprinkling of wood shavings covering her navy stable rug and peppered through her mane and tail.

'Hey, sweet girl,' says Joe.

The mare looks round from her haynet, her eyes calm and sleepy, and lets out a soft whicker. Lion is one of the horses bred by his father. She's nine years old now, and was born at two minutes before midnight on the evening before Joe's eighteenth birthday. Joe's dad said it was a sign that the two of them should be together, and gifted Joe the little chestnut filly for his birthday. She's the best present he's ever had.

Joe gives Lion a scratch on the forehead, just beneath her

chestnut forelock, and smiles as the mare nuzzles at his pocket, hopeful for a carrot. He duly obliges, feeding her a few pieces of carrot, and then sets about straightening up her rug.

Having sorted her rug, Joe checks Lion's water and then leaves her to snooze, exiting her stable and moving along the line to Pipplemouse. The skewbald gelding is already in his bed, having scraped all his bedding into a pile in the middle of the stable. He's sitting on top of it like a king on his throne. But he's a very sleepy king.

'Hey, boy,' says Joe, softly, as he unbolts the stable door.

Pipplemouse opens his eyes when he hears Joe, but the horse's eyelids are heavy, and when he realises Joe isn't bringing him any more hay his eyes quickly close again. He doesn't seem bothered about having a piece of carrot.

Doing his checks quickly, Joe exits Pipplemouse's stable and moves down the line to Truckle Bay. The gelding is dozing at the back of his stable, his bottom resting against the back wall, in his most favoured sleeping position.

'Hey, Truck,' says Joe, letting himself in.

The horse wakes with a start, then lets out a low whicker when he realises it's Joe. Truck's ears flick enthusiastically forward and he steps towards Joe, hoping for a tasty treat. Stroking the stocky gelding's neck, Joe feeds him a couple of pieces of carrot and then checks his rugs as he crunches the carrot happily. Once the rugs are done, he makes sure that the gelding still has some hay in his net and his water looks full.

'Sleep well, mate,' says Joe, giving the horse a forehead rub. 'We'll have some more fun tomorrow.'

Slipping out of the stable, Joe locks and double checks the bolts, and then turns to leave, almost colliding with someone coming along the passageway.

'I'm sorry,' he says, just before he registers the person is Ella. He grins. 'Oh, hi.'

'Joe, erm... Hi,' says Ella, blushing. 'I was just checking on the horses.'

'Snap,' he says, his grin getting wider before he realises he must look like some kind of Cheshire Cat, and promptly stops smiling.

Ella looks taken aback.

Joe groans inside. He must look and sound like an idiot. Why can't he just be cool? Now she's staring at him, waiting for him to say something, and suddenly he's tongue-tied.

He clears his throat. Why does this woman make him feel like a bumbling, nervous fifteen-year-old again? 'How are—'

Ella kisses him.

It takes a moment for Joe to respond. It's unexpected but not unwanted. Very much not unwanted. Pulling her closer to him, Joe kisses her back, fast and urgent.

He's not sure how long they spend like that, but at some point Truckle Bay snorts loudly at them, and gives Joe a poke with his muzzle, hoping for more carrot. It breaks the moment, and they laugh.

Joe duly obliges, feeding Truck a couple of pieces of carrot. Then, without saying anything, Ella takes him by the hand and leads him out of the stables and towards the lorry park.

~

As soon as they're inside the living area of Ella's horsebox, they're kissing again. Hungry, urgent kisses that tell Joe Ella wants this just as much as he does.

Unbuttoning his shirt, she pushes the fabric away from his skin. She kisses his chest, then runs her hands down to his breeches and starts unfastening his belt. She makes quick work of it, and before he knows it, he's naked aside from his socks.

'There's a bit of an imbalance here,' he murmurs, lifting her t-shirt over her head and unclasping her black lace bra.

He teases her nipples with his tongue as he undoes her breeches. She wriggles her hips and they slip down her legs so she can step out of them.

'There, that's a little more equal,' says Joe.

Groaning as Ella takes him in her hand, he kisses her again. He's rock hard and, as he presses his lips against hers, he feels her smiling.

'I want you,' he says, inhaling the lemony scent of her shampoo as he kisses her neck.

'I want you too,' replies Ella, her words quick and breathy.

Joe lifts her up and Ella curls her legs around his waist. He's at the point of no return, but he wants to be certain. He pauses, looking into Ella's eyes. 'You're sure?'

Her cheeks are flushed and there's lust in her eyes. She nods. 'Yes.'

Gripping her buttocks in his hands, Joe plunges into her. They move together, bodies in unison, pleasure pulsing through them. He wants to take his time, but she feels so great. He needs her too badly, too much, to slow down.

He kisses her neck. Thrusts harder, faster. 'You're amazing.'

'So good,' gasps Ella, pulling him closer, deeper. 'So good.'

They climax together, then, both of them breathless, climb up onto the bed in the Luton and curl up together under the duvet.

It takes barely two minutes for Joe to fall asleep.

FRIDAY

CHAPTER SEVENTEEN

ELLA

He's gone?

It's not even light yet.

From her vantage point in bed in the Luton, Ella peers through the gloom and around the living space of the lorry. There's no sign of Joe, and no sound of him in the tiny shower room.

Has he really just left?

She can't help but feel disappointed. It's barely six in the morning so she doubts that he *had* to go. Or, if he did, he could've woken her up to say goodbye. But no, it seems that he's chosen to sneak away without saying a word.

Ella sighs.

Maybe she was a fool to think he'd be better than that.

Lying back on the bed, she pulls the navy-and-white duvet up to her chin, closes her eyes and tries to push away all thoughts of Joe and get back to sleep. It doesn't work, though. The bed seems colder, less cosy, without him in it. And the chilly air in the lorry keeps her awake. In her mind's eye, she replays last night – that kiss, the way Joe used his hands, and the way he felt inside her.

She clenches her fists. Opens her eyes.

Get a grip!

Yes, okay, it was amazing, but it's over now. She was the one who made a move on him; they never promised each other anything. Now she needs to move on and focus on today's classes, not waste her time fantasising over some man. So he's run off without so much as a *'thanks for last night'*? Is she disappointed about that? Yes, for sure, but she needs to get over it.

After all, what did she really expect? Joe's the darling of the show jumping world, the sport's top pin-up. Realistically, it was only ever going to be a one-night thing.

Exhaling loudly, Ella contemplates getting up. She's wide awake now so there's no point staying in bed. If she gets up now, she can get an early start on the mucking out, then grab breakfast before she takes the horses for a leg stretch.

She flinches and pulls the duvet closer around her as the handle of the external door into the living area clicks down. The door opens.

What the...?

'Hey?' says Joe, smiling as he pops his head inside and sees her. 'You're awake.'

'I am,' says Ella, feeling her stomach flip as Joe steps into the lorry's living space and closes the door. 'I thought you'd done a runner.'

'Never,' says Joe, looking surprised. 'I woke up just after five so I ventured out and got breakfast to go from the café we went to yesterday. I hope that's okay?'

'That sounds great,' says Ella. 'It smells amazing too.'

Moving across the living space to the Luton, Joe passes Ella a takeaway coffee and a paper bag. 'Here you go.'

She takes them and sets the coffee down at the side of the bed before opening the bag. The bacon aroma hits her with its full force even before she's fully registered the contents.

She looks back at Joe, grinning. 'Coffee and a bacon buttie in bed? I think you might just be the perfect man.'

A flicker of something that Ella can't place flashes across Joe's expression before he smiles. 'I'm definitely not perfect, but I do my best.'

Ella takes a bite of the bacon roll and makes a satisfied noise. 'Well, your best is perfect enough for me. Are you going to stand there or come back up here?'

'I'm coming up,' says Joe, passing her his coffee and breakfast, and then kicking off his boots before climbing up into the Luton beside her.

As they sit together in bed, eating their bacon rolls and getting their first caffeine fix of the day, Ella thinks this might be the best breakfast, with the best company, she's ever had.

CHAPTER EIGHTEEN

WAYNE

It's super busy in the show's forge this morning. It's barely seven and Wayne's already made a new set of shoes for one of the Household Cavalry and nailed shoes back onto three show ponies who threw one in their early-morning exercise slot.

The pony he's just finishing up – a smart little Welsh Section C who is due to compete for the Mountain & Moorland championship later today – has been a right joker, pulling Wayne's gloves out of his back pocket while he's working, and then wiggling his top lip on the back of Wayne's neck and nibbling his hair while he's been doing the clenches. At least he's all done now.

Putting the pony's foot down, Wayne straightens up and rubs his lower back. He's fully recovered from his injury from earlier in the year, but every now and then he gets the odd annoying twinge. He turns to the pony's owner, a studious twelve-year-old with long plaits, and says, 'He's all done.'

She smiles gratefully. 'Thank you.'

'No problem,' says Wayne. 'And good luck in your class.'

As the pony is led out of the forge by his young owner, Wayne nips out too. He's desperate for a coffee and could do with a sugar hit as well. Megan's got another modelling meeting this morning – an exciting opportunity to work with another household brand – so she won't be joining him until later. He's having such a great time here with her, but he just wishes he hadn't blown the big moment he'd planned. He needs to think of another way to do it, and fast. It's already Friday and they'll be heading home on Sunday afternoon. The clock is ticking.

He reaches the coffee truck and orders the biggest coffee they do and a chocolate muffin, then stands and waits as the server prepares his order. Even though this truck is backstage, it's still super busy. There seems to be a constant queue at the refreshment trucks. While he waits, Wayne watches the competitors and grooms taking horses to and from the stables and the arenas, and members of the show crew in their branded polo shirts and sweaters bustling about moving props and getting things set up for the morning performance. Wherever he looks, the place is a hive of activity.

'Here you go,' says the barista, handing Wayne his coffee and muffin. 'Enjoy.'

'Thanks, mate,' replies Wayne. 'Have a good one.'

He takes a long slurp, smiling as the caffeine starts to do its magic, then makes his way back along the backstage passageways.

Stepping through the doorway into his forge, Wayne halts. He's surprised to see a large grey horse is already here.

'Hello?' says Wayne, frowning. 'Did I miss an appointment?'

'Hi, no, we don't have an appointment,' replies a twentysomething blonde woman with a low ponytail and wearing a Doug Wallingford Show Jumping Team-branded sweatshirt, blue jeans and yard boots who appears from around the other side of the horse. 'I'm Pippa. I work for Doug Wallingford. Sorry to just come right in, but Arthur was causing a bit of mayhem out in the passageway and the other farrier is busy.'

'No worries, Pippa,' says Wayne. 'How can I help?'

'He's managed to pull the nails out along one side of his off hind,' replies Pippa, nodding towards the horse's back foot. 'No idea how. It was fine last night but this morning the shoe was twisted and I found half the nails in his bed.'

'Okay, no problem,' says Wayne, setting his coffee and muffin down at the back of the forge and coming over to give the horse a friendly rub on his neck. 'Let's take a look.'

The big grey flinches as Wayne touches him. Wayne frowns. 'It's okay, mate. I just want to help you out with your shoe.'

The horse stands still but he flicks his ears back and eyes Wayne suspiciously.

'What's up? You seem rather on edge,' says Wayne, stroking the grey's neck a while longer. He needs to get the horse to chill out, so he prattles away to him, trying to communicate there's nothing to worry about. 'I'm quite friendly, mate. You don't need to worry, but I do need to take a look at your foot. Are you happy to let me do that?'

'Sorry, he can be a bit jumpy,' says Pippa with an apologetic expression.

'How is he usually to shoe?' asks Wayne, still stroking the horse.

'He's good. But he's generally quite mistrustful of humans, especially men.'

Wayne nods. It's not that uncommon, sadly. Horses have long memories; they remember if they've been given a scare or badly treated. Wayne keeps talking to the horse in a conversational tone and stroking the big grey's neck until the horse blows out and looks more relaxed. Once he does, Wayne runs his hand from the horse's neck, along his back and then down his hind leg. The horse duly obliges by lifting up his foot and letting Wayne hold it.

'Okay, boy, let's see what you've got going on,' says Wayne, brushing a few stray wood shavings from the inside of the horse's hoof so that he can get a better look. 'Ah, yeah, I see what you mean. It looks like he's stepped on the inside of the shoe and it's twisted the metal and pulled out the nails. He's taken a bit of hoof off but not so much that it'll cause him any problems. I should be able to tidy up his foot, repair the shoe and get it back on okay.'

'That's great,' says Pippa, although there's some reservation in her voice.

'Are you sure about that?' asks Wayne, curiously.

She avoids his eye contact. 'Yeah, well...'

Wayne puts the horse's foot down and steps across to his tools, selecting what he needs for the job before moving back to the grey gelding. He looks back at the horse's groom, trying to work out what the issue could be. 'What's going on? Do you want me to fix this?'

'Yeah, of course. It's just...' Pippa shrugs. 'It's just that Doug isn't getting along with Arthur. There've been a few incidents during the show, and Doug's pretty angry. I expect he'd have been happy to have an excuse for not competing Arthur. And that would've been better for Arthur too.'

As Wayne starts removing the horse's twisted shoe, he remembers Hattie telling them something about Doug having a fall off a grey horse in the warmup the other night. Maybe this is the one.

'That's a shame,' he says evenly. Then he pauses, waiting for the horse's groom to say more. He knows she will. They always do.

That's the thing about being a farrier: it's like being at the hairdressers – people are stuck in one place, having their hair done or waiting as their horse is shod, and it makes them talk to fill the silence.

'He's said poor Arthur is on borrowed time,' confides Pippa sadly. 'He's a good horse, Doug imported him from the US – paid a lot for him – but they've never got along. Since we arrived here, they've got even worse.'

'I'm sorry to hear that,' says Wayne, pulling out the last nail and removing the shoe. 'That's a shame.'

'Yeah. Doug is a dominant kind of rider and Arthur knows his own mind. They clash, and it doesn't end well.' She sighs. 'Doug doesn't always treat the horse well when people aren't watching. I think it'd be better for them both if he sells Arthur sooner rather than later, but he keeps banging on about not letting the horse get the better of him.'

'Sounds like he's letting his pride get in the way of what's right,' says Wayne, as evenly as he can. He hates any kind of bad treatment towards animals, and he can imagine what 'not treating the horse well' looks like – and that it's not at all pretty.

'Exactly that. It's typical Doug, so I've heard. I've only worked for him for a few months.' Pippa lowers her voice and moves closer to Wayne and Arthur. 'To be honest, I'm already looking around for my next job, but I don't want to leave poor Arthur.'

As Wayne fires up the furnace so he can heat up the iron shoe and reshape it to fit Arthur's hoof perfectly again, he hopes Hattie is able to find a way to help the grey gelding.

CHAPTER NINETEEN

HATTIE

Their early-morning exercise slot finishes in fifteen minutes, but that's fine with Hattie. She's done all she needs to with Pink Fizz and she's now just walking the spritely roan gelding around the outside of the international arena on a long rein, letting him relax and cool off.

As they walk, she watches Daniel cantering large, relaxed circles on The Rogue – impressed as always at how in tune the pair are together. She's smiling to herself when a less harmonious pairing catches her eye. Over in the far corner, Doug Wallingford is having problems with his grey gelding – Arthur V. The horse seems to have seen a monster lurking in the corner of the arena, over by some TV filming equipment, and is prancing, banana-ing his body away from the offending objects.

Doug is having none of it. He's heavy-handedly trying to yank the horse's head towards the spooky area, and Arthur is resisting. Hattie watches as the grey gelding throws up his head, almost smacking Doug in the face, then bounces on the spot before leaping away from the corner.

Doug, becoming more red-faced by the second, turns the horse sharply back towards the corner, forcing the gelding to face his fear again. This time, Arthur leaps into a half-rear, twisting sideways, again refusing to go into the corner.

'Approach and retreat would help him gain some confidence,' says Hattie, walking Pink Fizz in a circle nearby. 'He just needs a moment to see it's okay.'

Doug glares at her, keeping the gelding in trot and accelerating him around a circle and back into the corner again. 'Bugger off, will you. I know what's best for my own horse.'

She says nothing, watching as Doug continues to battle against Arthur; the horse's spooks and snorts are becoming more pronounced and louder by the minute. A few moments later, a particularly violent spook almost sends Doug flying out of the front door over the horse's head.

All the other riders in the arena have moved away from this end of the space, focused on their own horses and not wanting to get caught up in any drama. Hattie sees Daniel looking over at her, a worried expression on his face.

'I do know what I'm talking about,' says Hattie to Doug. 'I've worked with a lot of—'

'Bloody hell, you're a right nosy bitch, aren't you,' says Doug, spittle flying as he spits out the words. 'I'm not some bloody amateur. *I* know what I'm doing.'

'I'm not saying that you—'

'Will you pack it in,' growls Doug to the grey gelding, riding him back into the corner.

The horse responds with a forceful swerve sideways and a powerful fly buck, throwing Doug forward and almost over the gelding's head.

Swearing under his breath, Doug dismounts. He glares up at Hattie, his eyes narrowing, and says in a mean-spirited tone, 'If you think you're so bloody marvellous, why don't you try?'

Hattie's surprised – she never anticipated Doug would tell her to get on the horse – but she's certainly willing to see if she can help. She doesn't want the show jumper to hold Pink Fizz, though – the man's angry energy will do nothing for the highly strung gelding – so she beckons Daniel over.

Dismounting, Hattie crosses her stirrups over the saddle out of the way and hands Daniel Pink Fizz's reins. 'I'm just going to see if I can help Arthur; he's worried about the corner.'

'Okay,' says Daniel evenly.

Hattie knows Daniel saw what was going on, but he's tactfully staying out of the argument between her and Doug. He knows she doesn't need him to fight her battles, that she's perfectly capable of doing that herself.

She turns towards Arthur and Doug. 'Shall I take him?'

Doug looks at her dismissively. 'I expect he'll have you on the ground in less than a minute. He's strong-willed and bad-mannered, the sort who needs a man on him to show him who's boss.'

Hattie doesn't rise to the bait – after all, actions speak louder than any words can. She simply takes Arthur's reins and smiles sweetly at Doug. 'Thanks.'

'Do you want a leg up?' asks Doug, grudgingly.

'Not right now,' replies Hattie, her tone even. 'I'm just going to get to know him first.'

Doug shrugs and makes a scoffing noise.

Ignoring him, Hattie turns towards Arthur. First, she gives the big grey horse a rub between his eyes, waiting until the tension starts to leave him and he lowers his head. Then she runs up the stirrups on his saddle so they don't bang against his sides and undoes one side of the reins from the bit, making the reins into a makeshift long line. Leading the tall grey gelding towards the corner, she keeps the long rein loose and relaxed, letting the horse pick his own pace and how far he wants to go into the corner.

When he stops and eyes the TV equipment suspiciously, Hattie waits too. She strokes the gelding's neck and tells him he's a good boy. Then, as he becomes more relaxed, she asks him to turn away from the corner and walks him in a large loop, giving him time to lick and chew, exhaling the tension he's been holding.

The next time they approach the corner, Arthur seems more confident. He walks further into it, closer to the TV equipment that he's been convinced is a monster.

'Good boy,' says Hattie, rubbing his neck and feeding him a Polo from her breeches pocket. 'See how brave you are.'

Doug snorts with laughter somewhere behind them.

Again Hattie ignores him. She stands with Arthur, letting him chill out in the spot that was previously terrifying to him, and then, when she judges that the timing is right, she asks him to take a step closer to the TV equipment.

Arthur does as she asks.

'So brave,' says Hattie, feeding him another Polo. 'Good boy.'

Without her having to ask him, the horse takes another step closer to the equipment, and then another. Then he extends his neck and gently touches the piece of equipment closest to him with his muzzle.

'Clever boy,' says Hattie, giving Arthur another rub and a Polo.

The gelding is relaxed and happy. He now seems unbothered about the corner that he'd previously believed to be harbouring a monster. Giving him another neck rub, Hattie asks the horse to come alongside the arena boards, then climbs onto the top of them, puts down the stirrups, and gets into the saddle. Arthur stays perfectly still as she mounts.

Realising that the stirrup leathers are set far too long for her, Hattie crosses the stirrups in front of the saddle and rides Arthur in a relaxed walk circle without stirrups.

'Good boy,' she says, giving his withers a rub. 'So brave.'

They walk on a loose rein in a circle and then a figure of eight in and out of the previously spooky corner. Asking the gelding to trot, they trot a circle each way, and then repeat the same pattern in canter. Not once does the horse spook. Not once does he fight against Hattie.

Asking him to halt, Hattie rubs Arthur's neck and then reaches down to feed him a Polo. 'Good boy, so brave.'

The horse blows out, relaxed, happy and seemingly pleased with himself.

'All hail,' says Doug sarcastically, and he walks towards them doing a slow hand clap. 'Proud of yourself? Smug that you've shown me up, are you?'

Hattie frowns. Dismounting, she looks at Doug's angry red face. 'I just wanted to show you a way to get him okay with the corner that didn't involve forcing him into it.'

'You made me look like a bloody idiot,' Doug retorts, clearly furious as he snatches the grey gelding's reins from her, causing the horse to throw up his head. 'The pair of you did.'

'We didn't cause you to do anything,' says Hattie, her tone laced with steel. 'If you look like an idiot, you did that all by yourself.'

'Stupid bitch,' mutters Doug as he turns away, yanking Arthur's reins to make the horse follow him. As he's led away across the arena, the big grey gelding looks back towards Hattie several times, as if pleading with her to rescue him.

His expression breaks her heart.

CHAPTER TWENTY

JOE

The Christmas Cracker Relay competition is always one of Joe's favourites. He was pleased to be paired with Aimee Eastford and her speedster jumping mare, Zippy Fantastic, but less happy that they've been drawn last to jump in the competition.

It's been a long wait as each of the other pairs have taken their turn in the arena, and the course has been causing its fair share of difficulties. It's a relatively short track with just nine jumps, but it's big and twisty, and for some of the horses having another horse in the arena while they jump has proven a bit of a distraction. One or two pairs have had issues with passing the baton as well – with their horses, unaccustomed to having a short stick being handed between riders at the end of one round and the start of the other, spooking and costing them valuable seconds on the clock. Joe and Aimee have practised the hand-off a couple of times in the warmup, and so far so good.

Now they're next to jump.

Turning towards one of the warmup fences – an upright – Joe canters Pipplemouse to it and smiles as the skewbald gelding pops over neatly. He'd originally intended to ride Royal Lion this afternoon, but somehow she scraped her knee in the stable overnight and although she's sound, the knee is a bit puffy so he didn't want to risk it. Pipplemouse isn't a speedster like Lion, but hopefully they'll still be able to give it a good go.

'You ready?' asks Aimee as the steward beckons them across to the arena entrance.

'Yes, let's do this,' replies Joe, slowing Pipplemouse to a walk.

Riding across to the steward, Aimee and Joe follow the woman's instruction and enter the arena to the left, giving Doug Wallingford and Otto Schneider room to exit on the right.

'And last to go,' says the commentator, 'we have British number one Aimee Easton, riding TY Communications Zippy Fantastic, and Joe Broughton riding Baroness Lathenby's Pipplemouse.'

All around the arena, the crowds are cheering. Joe hears teenage girls, and a few boys, screaming his name and tries not to be distracted by all the 'I heart Joe Broughton' signs and banners that are being held up. There seem to be far more of them than yesterday.

Aimee looks at Joe and raises her eyebrows. Joe gives a self-depreciating smile and a small shake of his head. Aimee laughs.

The buzzer goes, and it's down to business. Joe takes his attention away from the audience and back on the job. A hush falls over the international arena.

As agreed, Aimee will jump first on Zippy Fantastic. As she asks Zippy to canter on, Joe moves Pipplemouse to the far end of the arena where the passing of the baton has to take place between their two rounds, and walks the gelding in large circles while they wait for their turn.

Aimee and Zippy Fantastic are fast, really fast. They whizz around the short course, flying the fences with ease and taking the shortest, fastest turns. As they near the second to last jump of their round, Joe shortens his reins, communicating to Pipplemouse that it's almost their turn. The skewbald gelding collects himself, feeling ready to spring into action as soon as Joe gives him the signal.

As Aimee and Zippy leap over the last, Joe steers Pipplemouse into position for the baton exchange. Aimee speeds through the finish towards them. Joe holds out his hand. Pipplemouse canters on the spot.

'Now it's time for the all-important passing of the baton,' says the commentator. 'Can they do it quickly?'

All around the arena, it feels as if the audience are holding their breath.

Pipplemouse isn't sure he wants Zippy cantering up to him, but Joe reassures the gelding and he holds a steady line, allowing Joe to extend his arm and take a firm grip on the baton as Aimee holds it out towards him.

The crowd cheers.

Aimee and Zippy return to a walk while Joe and Pipplemouse leap into action. They canter towards the first fence and clear it easily, then cut tightly back to the second and continue on at a decent pace over the next few fences.

Pipplemouse seems to be enjoying himself, but Joe's careful not to push the skewbald too fast as they reach the far end of the arena and jump the trickiest combination – a short-strided double of verticals – and then turn back the way they came.

There are just two more fences to go. Pipplemouse is jumping brilliantly.

'And they're up on the clock,' says the commentator, the excitement clear in his voice. 'Zippy Fantastic and Pipplemouse are the fastest so far.'

People are starting to applaud and shout encouragement. Joe feels Pipplemouse's attention waver from the job in hand to the crowd, but the skewbald gelding still manages to clear the penultimate fence and accelerate along the side of the arena towards the final jump.

'Cheer them on, boys and girls,' says the commentor. 'Show them you're behind them.'

The cheering gets even louder. People are stamping their feet on the floor of the stands and banging their hands against the railings.

Joe feels Pipplemouse tense. Pipplemouse isn't used to all this audience participation. He's a careful jumper, but the noise is rattling him.

'It's okay,' says Joe to the horse. 'Don't worry.'

As they speed towards the last fence, Pipplemouse suddenly spooks away from the grandstand where a group of teenagers have hung a huge 'I heart Joe' banner over the railings and are flapping it as they cheer them on.

'It's okay, it's okay,' Joe tells the horse. 'It won't hurt you.'

Pipplemouse isn't so sure.

Still, Joe manages to loop the skewbald back towards the last fence without crossing their tracks. There's a bright red Christmas cracker filler beneath it, which isn't something Pipplemouse usually bothers about, but he's spooked and has to jump it on an angle.

The skewbald gelding tries his heart out, but he doesn't quite get enough height to clear it cleanly. The toe of his near fore scrapes across the top pole. For a moment it seems like it's going to stay put, but then it rocks out of the jump cups and falls to the ground.

The crowd groan.

'And unfortunately that fence down has cost Aimee Eastford and Joe Broughton the win,' says the commentator, clearly disappointed. He injects some more enthusiasm into his voice. 'So that means that the winners of the Christmas Cracker Relay competition are Doug Wallingford riding Spicetown and Otto Schneider riding Maximus IV.'

'I'm really sorry,' says Joe to Aimee as they ride through the exit to leave the arena. 'All that noise really bothered him, and when those kids flapped that banner towards him he totally lost his concentration.'

'It happens.' Aimee shrugs, giving Joe a smile. 'Some days you lose. It's just a fun class anyway, nothing too serious.'

'Yeah,' says Joe, giving Pipplemouse's neck a rub. The horse tried his best even after being given a fright; you can't ask for any more than that.

But although Aimee's right, Joe still feels bad. He should've realised the commentator would try to whip the crowd up into a frenzy. He should've put ear covers on Pipplemouse and stuffed them with cottonwool so the noise wasn't so startling for the horse. He feels as if he's let both Aimee and the gelding down.

The collecting ring is busy, filled with competitors warming up for the next round of the eventers vs show jumpers league competition. Guiding Pipplemouse over to a quiet spot, Joe asks the gelding to halt and then gives the horse's neck a rub. 'I'm sorry, Pip.'

'Bad luck,' says Holly, his groom, coming over to them. She feeds Pipplemouse a treat, and throws a woollen rug over his quarters. 'All that cheering got to him.'

Joe nods. 'I should've asked you to put ear covers on him.'

'We'll know for next time,' says Holly. 'But those kids really shouldn't have been allowed to wave that banner. Poor Pip probably thought it was a great big ghost coming to attack him.'

'I know, right?' says Joe, dismounting and running his stirrups up before loosening the gelding's girth a notch. 'Any horse would've found it off putting.' He strokes the horse's neck again. 'Poor Pip, you tried your best.'

'He really did,' agrees Holly, taking the horse's reins over his head and feeding him another treat. 'I'll take him back to the stables while you walk the course for the next class. You've been drawn fifth to jump in the order, so I'll head straight back with Truck so you can warm up once you've walked.'

'Thanks, Holly,' says Joe. 'You're a star.'

'I know,' says Holly, grinning as she turns towards the stables. 'Come on, Pip. Let's get you washed off and back with your haynet.'

As Holly leads Pipplemouse away, Joe has some water from the bottle Holly brought him and leans against the fence as he waits for the eventers vs show jumpers course to be opened. In his mind, he runs through the round he's just jumped – replaying Pipplemouse's spook over and over, trying to figure out a way he could have anticipated it faster and supported the horse better to stay on his line towards that last fence.

'Hey, you okay?' asks Ella.

Joe looks up at her. He'd been so lost in replaying the round, he hadn't even seen her approaching. He forces a smile. 'I'm fine, I'm just…'

'It wasn't your fault,' says Ella. 'I was watching in the stands and all those banners and signs being waved about, and the roaring of the crowd? It was crazy. The commentator should've told the audience to stop that nonsense. It's no wonder poor Pipplemouse got scared.'

'I know, but I just think there must be something I could've done to—'

'There wasn't,' says Ella, decisively. 'So don't go beating yourself up over it.'

Joe stares at her. He's never told her what he gets like if he believes he could've performed better – given his horse a better experience – but she just seems to understand.

She really gets me.

Joe smiles. 'Thanks.'

'I didn't do anything,' she replies lightly. 'But I know what it's like to agonise about a mistake obsessively, and from the expression on your face as I was walking over here, I'm pretty sure you do too.'

'You're amazing,' says Joe, and without thinking, he pulls Ella to him and kisses her.

It's only as the flashbulbs go off around them that he realises their fledgling romance is now no longer a secret.

CHAPTER TWENTY-ONE

DANIEL

The eventers vs show jumpers competition doesn't go their way. Daniel and Pink Fizz jump a solid clear, as did Fliss, Imy and Jonathan, but Greta and her less-experienced horse, Triple Threat, has an unlucky stop at the third part of the combination, and Fergus and Dodger have a pole down over the water trays. The show jumpers have all been on great form, with Antonio, Clara, Fernando, Emma and Joe all jumping foot-perfect rounds, and just Doug and his big grey horse, Arthur V, having a fence down.

As they ride back into the international arena for the prize-giving, Daniel notices how upset Arthur looks. Unlike the other team horses who are walking calmly, the grey gelding is snatching at the reins and jigging. Doug, red-faced and clearly not happy with the horse but trying not to let it show to the audience, shortens his reins. The gelding throws up his head and then plunges forward in protest.

Daniel would rather keep well away from Doug, but the steward directs them into position for the prize-giving, lining up at the bottom end of the arena, facing the royal box. The luck, or lack of luck, of the draw means that Daniel is right alongside the show jumper and can hear the man swearing at his horse through gritted teeth.

'And now to the presentation of the prizes,' says the commentator. 'And in this fast-moving eventers vs show jumpers league competition, today has seen our show jumping team triumph.'

The commentator pauses while the people in the grandstands applaud.

'This afternoon, Mike Brightford, from one of our valued sponsors, Brightford Glazing, and his wife Fiona will be presenting the prizes, along with their daughter Annabel.'

As jazzed-up classical music plays, a fortysomething man in a tuxedo with an elegant lady in a long navy evening dress and a teenage girl in a pink prom dress step into the arena. They're accompanied by two members of the show crew, one carrying a basket of rosettes and the other a basket of carrots.

Approaching Joe Broughton, who is standing at the top of the line of show jumpers, the couple present him with his winner's rosette and then move along to Clara Philips and her piebald mare, Universal Pie.

While they wait, Pink Fizz stands quietly. His ears are pricked forward and his focus is one hundred percent on the girl in the prom dress as she lifts a carrot from the basket and gives it to Joe Broughton's chunky bay gelding, Truckle Bay.

Daniel chuckles. 'You'll get yours soon enough,' he tells the roan gelding, giving the horse's neck a rub. 'Just be patient.'

Beside them, Arthur V paws the ground vigorously.

'Pack it in, will you,' hisses Doug, tightening the reins yet again while also giving the horse a tap on the shoulder with his whip.

Daniel frowns, hating the way Doug is treating his horse. 'Maybe if you relaxed the reins, it'd help.'

'Back off,' growls Doug. 'No one asked you, or your stupid bloody girlfriend.'

As the prize-givers approach Doug, Daniel stays silent.

'And that's Doug Wallingford and his horse, Arthur V, getting their prize, completing the line up of the victorious show jumping team. The league competition, which is taking place each day of the show, currently stands at 2-1 to the show jumpers with just two more rounds to jump.'

Daniel accepts his second-place rosette from Mike and Fiona Brightford, and Pink Fizz is delighted to finally receive his carrot from their daughter, Annabel. He shows his happiness by giving Annabel a big carroty lick on her arm, making the teenager laugh.

'He likes you,' says Daniel, smiling at her.

'I like him too,' says Annabel, shyly. 'And he really likes carrots, doesn't he?'

'Yes, he does,' replies Daniel.

With a quick look at her parents to double check they're otherwise occupied, Annabel takes another carrot from the steward's basket and feeds Pink Fizz a bonus carrot.

Beside them, Doug tuts loudly.

'What's your problem?' asks Daniel once Annabel has moved on to the next horse.

'Your horse has no bloody manners,' scoffs Doug.

'My horse is just fine,' says Daniel firmly. 'You're the one here who's got no manners, the way you treat your horses...' Daniel shakes his head. 'I'm surprised you've not been disciplined yet.'

'You're out of your mind,' sneers Doug. 'I treat them right. I'm just not some rope-wriggling pony-patter like your girlfriend.'

'No, you overuse the whip and punish them with your hard hands,' says Daniel, with more than an edge of steel to his tone. 'I'm surprised they don't refuse to jump for you more often.'

'Oh, fuck off,' says Doug, his face reddening even more as Arthur's pawing gets faster, sending huge hoof-fuls of synthetic sand flying out behind him. 'This horse was fine until your girlfriend rode him this morning, but in the class this afternoon he's been a bloody nightmare. The stupid bitch has ruined him.'

Daniel feels rage building inside him. His jaw clenches. His eyes narrow.

Just who does this man think he is?

'Hattie isn't stupid or a bitch,' says Daniel, fiercely. 'And she's a better rider than you can ever hope to be. What's more, she treats all horses, all creatures to that matter, with respect. Unlike you.'

Doug opens his mouth to say more, but Daniel turns away, patting Pink Fizz's neck and looking instead towards Fliss, whose horse, Dark Matter, is standing on the other side of them.

Fliss meets his gaze and then glances towards Doug, rolling her eyes, clearly having heard every word of the exchange. 'What a dick,' she mouths at Daniel.

Daniel gives a nod. 'He's certainly that.'

'Oi,' says Doug, even more irritably and pointing his whip at Fliss. 'Don't you—'

Luckily, whatever he was going to say is drowned out by the commentator. 'And that's the prize-giving completed, so please put your hands together as our eventers and today's victors, the show jumpers, complete a lap of honour.'

As they canter around the outside of the international arena, 'Firework' by Katy Perry plays over the sound system. Pink Fizz canters calmly, not even bothered by the tails of his rosette fluttering around his face. Ahead of them, Arthur V seems to be getting increasingly wound up, plunging against Doug's hard hands and putting in a good few bucks and causing the audience to gasp.

As they complete the lap and exit into the collecting ring, Daniel knows one thing for certain. Hattie's right. Whatever else happens, that poor horse can't stay with Doug.

CHAPTER TWENTY-TWO

CANDICE

There's something rather delicious about hiding in plain sight. Candice has learned that over these past couple of months, and she's got really rather good at it. Practice makes perfect, after all, and she's certainly getting a lot of practice.

If she's honest, she hadn't been super thrilled about spending the week here at the London International Horse Show. It was her husband's idea rather than hers and, as a general rule, she prefers things to have been instigated by her. But he was so keen, so insistent, and when he promised to throw in trips to Harrods and Fortnum & Mason, and to book a suite at the Savoy, she relented and agreed to this little trip.

Candice had worried that the whole thing would be a huge bore, and that she'd have nothing much to do. But, as it turns out, she's found the whole thing a damn sight more interesting – revealing, if you like – than anticipated. Yes, she might not have wanted to spend the week this way, but now she's here she's really quite glad that she is.

'I got us another bottle,' says American tech mogul Arnold T. Gladstone, her husband of almost six weeks, as he tops up her champagne and holds the glass out to her. 'Here you go, honey.'

'Darling, thank you. What an angel you are,' she says in her cut-glass British accent, taking the glass. 'Whatever would I do without you?'

'You never need to worry about that, honey.' Arnold smiles and raises his glass to her. 'Your good health.'

Candice raises her own and clinks it against his. 'And yours, darling. And yours.'

After all, although at fifty-three she's no child, Arnold is over thirty years her senior and a lover of rich foods, fine wines and expensive cigars. If anyone needs to be hoping for continued good health, it's going to be him.

'So what do you fancy doing this evening?' asks Arnold. 'We could take in a show if you've had enough of the horses?'

From her vantage point in the VIP champagne bar up in the grandstand, Candice looks down at the eventers and show jumpers in the international arena receiving their prizes and shakes her head. 'Actually, darling, I'm fine staying here and watching some more,' she says sweetly to her husband. 'I know you enjoy it and we should make the most of being here, shouldn't we?'

Arnold looks pleased. 'Only if you're sure, baby?'

'I am,' says Candice, nodding. 'We could always book a late table at the Savoy Grill for afterwards. I know how you enjoy a good steak.'

'Well, that sounds swell,' says Arnold, grinning. 'You really are the most wonderful woman, Candy.'

Trying not to bristle at his use of her most hated abbreviation of her name, Candice takes a big sip of champagne and forces a smile. She's good at acting; the cards life has dealt her made it a necessity for survival. 'And I'm such a lucky woman to have found you, darling.'

Arnold reaches for her hand and kisses her palm. 'You're the love of my life.'

She looks into his eyes and thinks that he probably means it, although as she's actually his sixth wife these are no doubt words that he's said on many occasions before. Still, even though she's not the first, she is going to be his last wife – that, she is certain of. After all, if she was to leave him, the ironclad pre-nup he had her sign means she'd be leaving with nothing, and that just wouldn't do at all now, would it? No, of course not. So she's in this for the long run, sticking by him for as long as it takes.

Because Arnold T. Gladstone is worth billions.

CHAPTER TWENTY-THREE

WAYNE

Wayne feels just as awkward in his rented tux as he does in this five-star uber fancy hotel, but he tries to fake confidence for Megan's sake. He'd feel much more at home in his smartest jeans, but this evening is important to Megan and so he'll cope with few hours of discomfort to be here supporting her. And at least he has his mask to hide behind.

Megan looks stunning in a long, strapless red dress and with her hair swept up into a glamorous chignon. Her gold mask hides the top half of her face, but her eyes are as beautiful as always, and the red lipstick she's wearing tonight is extremely sophisticated.

'You okay?' she asks, putting her hand on his shoulder. 'I know this isn't your kind of thing.'

'I'm good,' replies Wayne, smiling. 'It's all for an important cause.'

'It is,' says Megan, smiling back at him. She takes his hand. 'Ready?'

Wayne adjusts his own gold mask so it's not pinching the top of his nose, then nods. 'As I'll ever be.'

They walk along the hotel hallway to the entrance of the

grand ballroom and give their names to the uniformed hotel staff on the door. They wait as the taller of the two men checks the guest list on his tablet. Finding their names, he taps the screen, then looks up at them.

'Welcome to the SARP inaugural masked ball,' he says in a plummy accent as he gestures for them to enter the ballroom.

'Thanks, mate,' says Wayne, and he and Megan move inside.

Survivors Against Revenge Porn, or SARP as they're more commonly known, reached out to Megan about a month ago. Although Megan's experience hadn't been specifically revenge porn, they'd felt that in talking about her own experiences, she'd helped a number of women who had experienced it, and invited her to be a SARP ambassador. Megan had been keen to get involved, and this charity masked ball is the first event she's attended. Neither of them are a hundred percent sure what to expect.

'Woah,' says Wayne, as they walk into the grand ballroom. 'This is…'

'Gorgeous,' says Megan, finishing his sentence.

She's right. The ballroom is like nothing he's ever seen before. The vast space is flanked by white stone pillars topped with gold cornicing, and along one side the massive floor-to-ceiling windows are framed with gold curtains. The floor is stone with hand-painted floral embellishments, and hanging from the ornately corniced ceiling are several of the biggest chandeliers imaginable.

Lavish flower displays cascade from huge vases that must stand at least five feet tall. There's a stage at the far end of the room, a dance floor and at least twenty or thirty tables of ten laid for dinner filling the space between the edge of the dance floor and where he is. The whole thing looks like something from a glossy magazine or an Instagram photo on some celebrity's grid.

Wayne feels even more ill at ease in his hired tux. He wishes he was in his local, the Red Lion, having a quick pint and a game of pool with Megan and the lads.

As if sensing his nerves, Megan grips his hand tighter. 'It'll be okay. We can do this.'

Wayne meets her gaze and smiles. He'd do anything for this woman. Wearing this tux and feeling awkward at this ball is nothing. 'Totally.'

They find their table just as they're asked to take their seats. The food is amazing and the people they've been sat with are all pretty fun. After a couple of glasses of wine, Wayne's feeling much less self-conscious and Megan seems to be enjoying herself.

After dinner, there are speeches and the results of the silent auction are announced. Then the lights are dimmed and the band start playing. As the dance floor gradually fills up, Wayne wonders if there's a way to propose here, tonight. He's got the ring with him – lately he's taken to carrying it everywhere. And this is certainly one of the most stunning and lavish buildings he's ever seen – it would make a lovely backdrop to a proposal, but it's too crowded in here.

He looks at Megan. 'Shall we go and get some fresh air on the terrace?'

'Sure,' Megan says, pushing her chair back from the table.

Hand-in-hand, they walk across the ballroom to the doors out onto the rooftop terrace. The night air is crisp and chilled, with a hint of frost. Wayne removes his tux jacket and puts in around Megan's shoulders.

'Thanks,' she says. 'Wow, look at this – the view is amazing.'

'It is,' says Wayne, following Megan's gaze. From here, on the terrace, there's a great view across the Thames. Below them, stretching out into the distance, the festive lights along the river-bank, and the lights of the boats cruising through the water, make London look magical. 'So pretty.'

They stand with their arms around each other, looking out

across the river. In the icy air, their breath plumes around them like smoke, and from inside the ball room they hear the fast tempo music fading into a slower, romantic ballad of a tune.

Maybe this is the moment?

Wayne checks the ring is in his top pocket, relieved when he feels the familiar outline of it inside a folded hankie.

I'm going to do it.

His heart rate accelerates as he slowly turns towards Megan, ready to go down on one knee.

'Megan, there you are!' booms a kindly-looking fifty-something woman in an elegantly tailored black tuxedo, hurrying over to them. 'There's a few people here really keen to meet you.'

Wayne and Megan turn back towards the doors onto the terrace and see a group of young women spilling through them.

'We've been looking all over for you,' says a woman in a pink dress and heels. 'We just wanted to say hi.'

'What you did, standing up to those men like you did, it was an inspiration,' says another young woman in a long, flowing, pale gold dress.

'Thank you,' says Megan. 'It's lovely to meet you all.'

As Megan chats with the group, Wayne tries not to let his disappointment show. The moment to propose has gone. He's missed it again. At the rate he's going, he wonders if he's ever going to manage to ask her, but he tries not to let how he's feeling show.

'Would you like to dance?' asks Wayne, after the group have gone back inside. He likes a bit of a dance and it's a good way to chase away the blues.

'No,' says Megan.

Wayne frowns. Megan usually loves to dance. In fact, she's looking at him a bit funny. 'What is it?' he asks.

She kisses him, then whispers in his ear playfully, 'Come with me.'

With his hand in hers, Wayne leaves the rooftop terrace and

allows Megan to lead him through the ballroom and out into the hallway. He's confused. 'Are we leaving?'

'Not yet,' says Megan, a mischievous smile on her lips. 'I've got something to show you.'

'Okay,' says Wayne, continuing to follow her, still none the wiser.

She leads him along the corridor, away from the grand ballroom and towards the loos. But they don't get that far. Instead, Megan pauses outside a door with a sign saying 'Staff Only'. She checks the corridor is empty, then pushes down the door handle.

Wayne's eyes widen. 'What are we...?'

Smiling, Megan pulls him inside. The room is the size of a small bedroom but rather than being made up for guests, it's being used to store equipment. On the other side of the room, there's a pair of French doors and a Juliette balcony.

'I found it when I was looking for the loos,' says Megan. 'I forgot to put in my contact lenses so I couldn't read the sign properly.'

'Okay,' says Wayne, still not sure why they've come here. 'So what did you want to show me?'

'This,' says Megan, giving him an impish smile. She reaches behind her and, in the next moment, the skirt of her red dress has detached from the corset bodice and drops to the floor.

'Wow,' says Wayne, taking in the sight of her. 'You look incredible.'

'Then fuck me,' she says.

'Here?' asks Wayne, surprised but already feeling his dick hardening.

'Against the balcony.' Megan turns and walks across to the French doors. Pulling them open, she steps up to the black iron railings of the Juliette balcony, then looks over her shoulder at him. 'Here.'

Wayne doesn't need to be told twice. She looks amazing, unreal even, in just her high heels, lacy thong, red corset and gold mask. Rushing across the room, he pulls her to him and kisses her deeply.

Megan returns the kiss, then turns around and presses her arse against him. Wayne groans. He can't get enough of this woman. Undoing his trousers, he pulls Megan's thong aside and thrusts into her. She grips the iron railings and pushes back towards him, helping him get deeper.

'So good,' she moans.

'Oh God, yes,' replies Wayne.

She feels incredible – and that, combined with the rebelliousness of being in a space they shouldn't be, looking out over the Thames illuminated in its festive lights, and the icy air nipping at his skin, makes Wayne unable to hold back any longer.

He thrusts harder, faster, until they cum loudly and together, then collapse into giggles at the absurdity of what they've just done and where they've just done it.

As he kisses Megan again, Wayne thinks to himself, *It doesn't get any better than this.*

CHAPTER TWENTY-FOUR

HATTIE

Watching the Shetland Pony Grand National is the best fun. Hattie and Daniel lean forwards in their seats in the riders' area of the grandstands, willing the young jockeys on as they hurtle around the course of miniature steeple-chase fences, which have been positioned around the outside track of the international arena.

With just one more lap to go, number six, a chestnut pony and their rider wearing yellow and green colours, and number two, a bay pony whose rider is wearing navy with pink stars, have moved ahead of the pack and are battling in out neck and neck.

'Look at them move,' says Daniel. 'It's remarkable.'

'Their little legs,' says Hattie, amazed at how fast the Shetlands can gallop. 'They're really going for it.'

All around the grandstands, the audience are cheering the ponies on and calling out their favourites, urging them faster.

'Come on number two,' shouts Daniel.

'Go, go, go number six,' calls out Hattie.

The ponies seem to respond, both putting on an extra burst of speed as they fly over the last fence and make the turn up the centre of the arena towards the finishing post.

'And it's too close to call as Highland Daredevil and Supersonic Bean gallop towards the finish,' says the commentator, his words fast and furious in true racing style. 'These two ponies are on superb form. And they're both determined to win. Is Highland Daredevil inching ahead? Is Supersonic Bean edging past?

The ponies dash towards the finishing line, their young jockeys crouched low over their necks.

'They're almost at the finish now,' continues the commentator. 'Just a few more strides to go. Who's going to win this? Who will be our winner?'

Highland Daredevil and Supersonic Bean fly through the finish, still neck and neck.

'It's impossible to tell!' shrieks the commentator. 'It's a photo finish.'

The rest of the ponies in the race streak down the centre of the arena and through the finish.

'Our first and second might not be confirmed yet, but we've got number three, Lipstick Lizzie, finishing in third place, and number nine, Magical Mystery Meg, finishing in fourth,' says the commentator.

The ponies all drop back to a walk. Their young riders are gleefully patting their ponies as their grooms – who are most likely their parents – rush over to congratulate them.

'And the result of the photo finish is in,' says the commentator. 'Again, it was incredibly close – the closest finish I think we've seen here at the London International Horse Show – but I can now announce that our winner of tonight's Shetland Pony Grand National is number six, Supersonic Bean ridden by Isabelle Francis, and in second we have number two, Highland Daredevil ridden by Zack Browne.'

The crowd cheers.

'Yay,' says Hattie. 'That winning pony has the best name.'

Laughing, Daniel nods. 'It does.'

Hattie grins as Daniel puts his arm around her. Then,

suddenly, she feels a chill go up her spine. She has the sudden feeling that someone is watching them.

She looks back towards the arena where the crew are speedily removing the mini steeplechase fences and getting the space set up for the Shetland Pony Grand National prize-giving. Everyone in the arena is busy – carrying sections of the fences, driving the tractor and trailer that they're getting loaded up onto, or setting out the huge urns of flowers which the ponies will line up between to receive their prizes. No one is looking towards the audience.

But as the hairs rise on the back of her neck, Hattie still feels as if someone's eyes are on her.

Weird.

Daniel doesn't seem to have noticed. 'Jingle Bells' has started playing over the speakers, and his focus is on the international arena where the Shetland ponies are now entering once again, this time to collect their rosettes from the sponsor of the class.

But Hattie can't relax enough to watch them. Instead, she slowly scans the crowds in the grandstands. There are so many people here, but none of them are looking towards her – they all seem to be watching the ponies, chatting with each other, and eating takeaway food from one of the many food stands. Having searched the crowd as much as she can, she takes a final glance across towards the VIP Phoenix Club seating on the other side of the arena entrance from the rider's area where she and Daniel are.

That's when Hattie sees her. While the distinguished-looking older man beside her is avidly watching the prize-giving, the ice-blonde-haired woman he's with is staring directly at Hattie. No, scratch that, she's glaring towards her.

Hattie feels adrenaline flood through her. She's never seen the woman before.

Who is she? Why is she staring?

For a moment, they look into each other's eyes, then the woman grimaces and turns away.

Hattie lets out a ragged breath.

'You okay?' asks Daniel, concern in his eyes.

'I... Yes, I...'

'What is it?'

Hattie shakes her head. She looks back towards the blonde woman, who is now laughing with the man beside her, then back at Daniel. 'Maybe it's nothing, but ever since we got here I've been getting these weird feelings that someone's watching me. I got the feeling again just now, and then I noticed that a woman over there in the VIP area was staring right at me.'

'Where?' asks Daniel.

Hattie points out the woman with the ice-blonde hair. 'Her.'

Daniel squints towards the woman. Shakes his head. 'I don't recognise her.'

'Me neither,' says Hattie. 'But she was definitely staring.'

'Maybe she's a fan of yours.'

Hattie laughs. 'As if! It's far more likely she's one of yours.'

Daniel shrugs. 'Maybe, but, you know, I've had a few weird "is someone watching me?" moments while we've been here too.'

'So maybe she's watching us both,' says Hattie, frowning. 'That's a bit worrying.'

Daniel looks again at the blonde woman. 'She could be, although she's not right now.' He looks thoughtful. 'Maybe it's just that different people are recognising us and staring, and we're not used to it. I mean, this environment is a million miles away from the rolling fields of the eventing world.'

Hattie nods. Daniel's right; she's thought the same herself. And there's no reason for a show VIP to be following them around and watching them. The idea is ridiculous really. She smiles at Daniel. 'You're probably right.'

And she knows he is. But, as she glances across to the VIP

with the icy blonde hair who is no longer paying them any attention, Hattie still feels uneasy.

CHAPTER TWENTY-FIVE

ELLA

After a win for Joe and a third place for Ella in the Christmas Snowman Stakes, they settle the horses down for the night, then grab Chinese food to go and take it back to Joe's hotel room. Sitting on his sofa, they eat as they replay the course and how their horses jumped, comparing notes and experiences. Ella smiles; it all feels so natural with Joe, as if she's known him for years rather than days.

'That turn you did between three and four was genius,' says Joe, eating his chicken chow mein out of the carton. 'I wish I'd thought of it.'

Ella laughs. 'You didn't need it – you were fastest anyway.'

Joe looks bashful. 'But I could've been faster. You'll be beating me soon with moves like that.'

'Maybe, but not today,' says Ella, taking a mouthful of lemon chicken and rice. 'My right-handed turns aren't as good as my left. I need to work on them.'

'You look good to me from all angles,' says Joe.

Ella throws a spare packet of chopsticks at him. 'Perv.'

He laughs and puts his hands up. 'Guilty as charged. Speaking of pervs, have you had any more hassle from your ex?'

'No,' says Ella, shaking her head. 'Not since I told him if he kept on harassing me I'd call the police, and then changed my number. Hopefully that's the last I ever hear from him.'

'Hopefully,' says Joe. 'He's clearly a dick.'

'A total dick,' agrees Ella. Pleased that after weeks of torment from Henry she's now able to think about it without feeling tearful. 'Thanks for being a good mate.'

Joe smiles. 'Anytime.'

They eat their food in a companionable silence, the rigours of the day starting to take their toll and lull the pair towards sleep. When they've eaten all they can manage, Joe takes the empty containers and puts them outside the door so the food smell doesn't linger in the room. It's a nice hotel and the room is large and airy, but it's very shades of grey and impersonal. Ella's always liked her living spaces to be more colourful, and although the room is a lot less cramped she kind of misses her lorry.

The thought doesn't last long.

Having taken out the takeaway cartons, Joe comes back into the room. He's got a glint in his eye, a mischievous look.

'What?' says Ella, a smile playing at her lips. 'Why are you looking at me that way?'

'I was just thinking I could do with some dessert,' replies Joe.

'Is that right?' says Ella, her tone playful. 'It's a shame we didn't get any.'

'On the contrary,' says Joe, moving across the room to her with an intense look on his face. 'I think we've got everything we need right here.'

'How so?' asks Ella, frowning and pretending she doesn't understand.

'Well, you see right here,' says Joe, kissing her lips, 'we've got the sweetest strawberries.'

Ella kisses him back, desire flaring inside her. 'Mmmmm nice, and what else?'

Joe follows up with light butterfly kisses across her jaw and down her neck. 'And just here, we've got delicious peaches and cream.'

'Oh yes?' says Ella, struggling to keep her tone even as the need for him surges through her.

Pulling her jumper off over her head, and undoing her bra, Joe kisses her from her collarbone to her nipple. 'And here we've got the most wonderful berries.'

She gasps as his tongue circles her nipple, crying out as he takes it in his mouth and sucks hard. Damn, she needs this man inside her. She needs him now.

She tries to remove his shirt, but he gently removes her hands. 'Not yet,' he tells her, softly. 'I haven't finished my dessert yet.'

Slowly, Joe undoes her breeches, then pushes them and her pants down as he kisses across her stomach, past her belly button, and beyond. He sinks to his knees.

'And here,' he says pushing two fingers inside her, 'is the most amazing passion fruit I've ever tasted.'

As he puts his mouth on her, and his tongue works its magic, Ella leans back against the wall for support and forgets everything else.

She's lost in the moment. In the feeling.

She never wants to be anywhere else.

SATURDAY

CHAPTER TWENTY-SIX

JOE

Joe wakes to find over two hundred notifications on his phone's lock screen. Ella's still fast asleep, snuggling against him, so he taps on the notifications and opens up X one-handed. The pictures taken by the press yesterday are trending – with online articles on several of the tabloids' websites and in the equestrian media. #showmance is trending on X and there are already several memes of the kiss being shared.

He scrolls through the comments he's been tagged in.

HORSEGIRL126

Noooooooooo! #pickmeJoe

CANTERINGFREE

Who's the bitch he's with???

OATSGRASSSUN

Don't worry it's just a #showmance

PONYMAD168

Is that Ella Cooper? WTAF??

POLESGUY

Ella 4 Joe. Bets on how long that'll last?? I say a week max

OVERWEGO88

HANDS OFF MY MAN, ELLA!!!

PONYMAD168

@PolesGuy less – two days tops!

POLESGUY

@PonyMad168 hahahahaha

Joe stops scrolling. He's always hated his 'pin up' status – as his dad used to refer to it – and the attention it brings. It's one of the reasons why he hardly ever dates; that, and because all he's ever wanted to do is to focus on training and competing with his horses.

Although now, he thinks, putting his phone face down on the bedside table and watching Ella breathing softly in her sleep, perhaps he does want something more. Ella is special. She gets him, and he thinks he gets her. He enjoys being with her and the connection they have; it's more... it's deeper, than he's experienced before.

Ella's eyelids flutter open.

'Hey you,' says Joe, reaching out and stroking her face.

She smiles, pretending to try and nip his fingers. 'Hey yourself. What time is it?'

'Early,' replies Joe as he picks up his phone. 'We're trending on X.'

Ella's eyes widen. 'Us? Why?'

'The press have posted those pictures taken of us together yesterday,' says Joe.

'The kiss?' asks Ella.

Joe nods.

'Oh God,' says Ella. 'I bet all your admirers are slaughtering me.'

Joe grimaces. 'They're not at all happy.' He strokes her face again, then pulls her closer for a kiss. 'But I am, I'm extremely happy, so bugger what they think.'

Ella smiles. 'Totally. I'd just better wear my hard hat when I go onto the showground, in case they try to throw stuff at me.'

'I'll protect you,' says Joe.

'I can protect myself, thanks,' says Ella, laughing. Kissing him, she slides her hand down his stomach and takes him in her hand. Unable to hold back, Joe pulls her on top of him and enters her. As she rides him hard, he knows one thing for sure.

The haters are wrong. This is more than a showmance.

CHAPTER TWENTY-SEVEN

WAYNE

He's on an early shift in the forge this morning and needs all the caffeine he can get. Problem is, it's been busy so far, so other than his first coffee of the day, he's not had the opportunity to get another. Having just finished replacing a lost shoe on one of the show hacks, and with no one else queuing, Wayne sees his chance to get a drink. Quickly unbuckling his chaps, he hangs them on a hook in the corner and heads towards the exit out towards the stables and the closest coffee van.

He almost runs straight into a large roan horse being led towards his forge.

'Space for a quick refit?' asks Hattie, peering under the horse's neck. 'Fizz has done something weird to his near fore shoe.'

'Sure,' says Wayne, trying not to let his disappointment show in his voice. Hattie's a mate so of course he's not going to turn her away, but he really is feeling knackered after the late night at the ball and the early start this morning.

'You're a lifesaver,' says Hattie, leading the roan gelding into the forge. She holds up her other hand. In it is a cup holder containing two tall takeaway cups. 'I brought you coffee; figured you might need it.'

Wayne feels his spirits lifting. He puts his hand on his chest. 'You, mate, are the lifesaver.'

Tying Fizz to the tie ring in the forge, Hattie hands Wayne one of the takeaway coffees. 'This is yours. Three sugars, just as you like.'

'Perfect,' he says, taking the cup and immediately drinking a few large gulps. It's hot, almost too hot, but he doesn't care. As he swallows the coffee down, he can almost feel himself becoming more energised. Putting the cup down beside his anvil, he collects his chaps from the hook and buckles them back into place. 'Thank you.'

'You're welcome,' says Hattie. 'How was the ball?'

'It was okay,' says Wayne evenly, as he picks up the roan gelding's front foot and takes a look at his shoe. 'Very posh, so not really my thing, but the food was nice and Megan enjoyed it.' He stays quiet about the bit he most enjoyed – the over-the-balcony sex in a staff-only room. He's never been one to kiss and tell, even in his most laddish days before Megan. Everyone deserves respect.

'Sounds good,' replies Hattie, giving Pink Fizz a stroke on his neck.

'Yeah,' says Wayne, nodding.

Hattie cocks her head to the side. 'But?'

Busted, thinks Wayne. Using his tools, he removes the gelding's shoe, then puts the horse's foot down and straightens up, exhaling hard. 'Look, if I tell you something, I need you to keep it quiet, okay?'

'Of course,' says Hattie, her tone curious. 'I'm a vault.'

'Right,' says Wayne. 'So, look, I want to propose to Megan.'

Hattie claps her hands together. 'Oh my God, that's amazing. I'm so excited for you.'

'Thanks,' says Wayne, turning on the furnace and placing Pink Fizz's shoe inside to heat up.

Hattie frowns. 'You don't seem very excited about it?'

'I was,' says Wayne, taking another large gulp of his coffee. 'But every time I've tried to propose, something happens to stop me. I had it all planned out a couple of nights ago. I took Megan to a fancy restaurant with great food and a stunning view, I wore a suit and there was champagne on ice, you know? The whole works. But then, just as I was going down on one knee, some fans recognised her and came over to us. After that, the moment was gone.'

'So you just need to pick another time,' says Hattie, finding a Polo in her pocket and feeding it to Pink Fizz.

'I did, last night on the terrace at the ball,' says Wayne, sighing. 'The view was magical out across the Thames, but, again, we got interrupted.'

Hattie looks sympathetic. 'That's tricky. Maybe you need to do it in a less public place?'

'Yeah,' says Wayne. 'But where? Everywhere around here is public.'

'So do it when we're back home.'

Wayne shakes his head. 'I want to do it somewhere different. Special.'

Looking thoughtful, Hattie takes a sip of her coffee. Then she smiles. 'I've got an idea. It's incredibly public – as public as it's possible to be, in fact – but I can practically guarantee Megan won't be recognised and you should be able to propose without interruption. Plus, it'll probably be captured on camera.'

'That would be amazing,' says Wayne. 'But how? Tell me.'

And so she does.

CHAPTER TWENTY-EIGHT

DANIEL

It's neck and neck with both teams so far having had just one fence down as the last four horses in the eventers vs show jumpers competition prepare to jump. The warmup area is less crowded now, which suits The Rogue, with just Fliss and Dark Matter, Antonio and Banyania XI, and Doug with Bright Spark III sharing the space.

Fliss jumps first. It's hard to know how things are going when you're in the collecting ring without a view of the arena, but Daniel's happy not to hear any falling poles or loud gasps from the audience, both of which would indicate faults being incurred.

As the crowd breaks into applause, the commentator says, 'And that's a solid clear round from Fliss Moreton and her great little mare, Dark Matter.'

Next up is Antonio de Luca. As he rides into the international arena, Daniel hears his young stallion, Banyania XI, give a loud snort. Moments later, Fliss exits the ring on a very jazzed-up Dark Matter.

'Everything okay?' asks Daniel, walking The Rogue closer to where Fliss is trying to calm the black mare.

'Yeah, fine,' says Fliss. 'She jumped like a dream, but as we were approaching the exit, Antonio's horse kind of lurched towards her. It freaked her out a bit.'

As Fliss continues to settle the mare, Daniel circles away and asks The Rogue to canter. They have a last pop over the practice fence and, as he comes back to a walk, Daniel strokes the bay's neck. 'Good lad. Let's go and have some fun, shall we?'

The Rogue blows out hard, as if to say, 'Yes, please.'

Daniel turns him towards the entrance. Antonio's round must be almost finished and they're next. He flinches as he hears the sound of wood crashing into wood from the international arena. Next moment, the bell rings. That's not good. A bell ringing either means a fence has been knocked down in a refusal and needs to be rebuilt, or that the horse and rider have been eliminated.

Next moment, he gets his answer as Antonio and his spritely stallion, Banyania XI, exit the arena. Antonio's shaking his head, disappointed.

'What happened?' asks Daniel.

'He didn't want to jump tonight,' says Antonio philosophically. 'His mind was not on the job. He would prefer to chase Fliss's mare instead. Once he got back to this end of the arena, he decided he wasn't keen on travelling back away from the collecting ring.'

'Sorry to hear that,' says Daniel. 'He looked on great form earlier.'

'He has all the talent,' says Antonio, giving the horse's neck a rub. 'But he has yet to learn to fully focus. I think mixing competition and stud work this summer has confused him. I will devise a better plan for next year.'

Daniel nods, and walks The Rogue to the entrance of the arena. Following the steward's instruction, he enters and stays to the left, walking The Rogue between the fences as the arena crew finish rebuilding a grey wall made of lots of wooden blocks. Daniel guesses that was the fence where Banyania XI decided to throw in the towel.

'And I'm afraid that was elimination for Antonio de Luca and Banyania XI,' says the commentator in his plummy voice. 'Which puts the show jumpers at a rather considerable disadvantage as the elimination adds 20 faults to their scorecard. Next to jump is the last rider on the eventers team, Daniel Templeton-Smith and his Badminton-winning horse, The Rogue.'

As the bell rings to indicate for Daniel to start the course, he asks The Rogue to canter. They pop neatly over the first two fences, then make a smooth turn back to a narrow jump with red-and-green poles and a filler in the shape of a Christmas jumper, before turning again to an upright gate followed by a double of oxers with Christmas cracker fillers beneath them. The Rogue makes easy work of them and canters on eagerly towards the water tray, and then loops back towards the grey wall that ended Antonio and Banyania XI's round. There's no such trouble for The Rogue, who flies over the wall and canters on towards the final triple.

'Steady,' says Daniel, as The Rogue tries to get a bit faster than he'd like.

The big bay responds, shortening his stride and popping neatly through the treble without touching a pole. As they canter through the finish, the crowd breaks into applause.

'And that's a copybook clear from Daniel Templeton-Smith and The Rogue,' announces the commentator. 'So the eventers finish with a penalty score of just four faults, making them the clear winners of tonight's competition.'

As The Rogue slows to a walk, Daniel drops his reins and gives the gelding a neck rub with both hands. 'Excellent work, boy,' says Daniel, grinning. 'You're a star.'

The Rogue gives a snort, as if to say, 'Of course I am.'

They pause before exiting, waiting to allow the last rider, Doug Wallingford with Bright Spark III, to enter the arena. Doug looks grim-faced, probably because no matter what he does, the show jumpers can't win tonight. He ignores Daniel as he trots past.

Fine, thinks Daniel as he rides The Rogue out into the collecting ring. Once a dick, always a dick.

'Well done, that was brilliant,' says Hattie, hurrying over to Daniel and The Rogue. She loosens Rogue's noseband and feeds him a piece of ginger biscuit. 'What a clever boy you are.'

'Thanks,' says Daniel, jumping off the gelding. He runs up his stirrups and loosens the girth. 'Wasn't he a total star?'

'Absolutely,' says Hattie, laughing as Rogue nuzzles her pockets, asking for more biscuits. 'And he knows it.'

'Always,' says Daniel, smiling as Rogue eats more biscuits and then holds up his top lip.

From the international arena, they hear cheering. The commentator says, 'And that's a foot-perfect round from Doug Wallingford and Bright Spark III, but it still doesn't change the result of the eventers vs show jumpers competition tonight – our winners are the eventer team and we'll be presenting them with their prizes very soon.'

~

Five minutes later, as they gather in the collecting ring to enter the international arena for the prize-giving, Daniel finds himself next to Doug Wallingford, who seems to be in an uncharacteristically jovial mood.

'Good round,' says Daniel.

'Thanks,' replies Doug, giving his stallion a pat on the neck. 'Makes a difference to ride something with a good attitude.'

Daniel picks up on the dig at the grey gelding, Arthur V. 'Where's Arthur tonight?'

Doug's expression clouds. 'In his bloody stable. I'm selling the creature. I'm done with its unreliability and histrionics. Bill Dartmouth is interested; we just need to haggle the price.'

Daniel says nothing. Trainer Bill Dartmouth is notorious for his abusive training methods. Hattie's going to be distraught when he tells her the man is in negotiations to buy Arthur.

CHAPTER TWENTY-NINE

CANDICE

The prize-givings are usually super dull, but this one has a little more attraction. Firstly, there's the fact that tomorrow, at the last competition of the eventers vs show jumpers league, she's going to be one of the people going out into the arena to present the prizes. One of Arnold's tech companies has sponsored the class, and he's very excited about getting to step out into the spotlight.

And secondly, the prize ceremony for this particular class is rather more appealing than those of some of the other classes. There's a particular rider, one of the eventers, who has the most chiselled-looking jawline and handsome good looks.

Candice has found she just can't keep her eyes off him.

Peering down into the international arena from her vantage point at the VIP champagne bar, Candice watches as the horses and riders line up between two lavishly decorated Christmas trees to await their rosettes. The eventers are the winners this afternoon, and the rider she has her gaze set on looks as calm and noble as always atop his large brown horse. She watches as he chats easily to the female rider on a black horse standing along-side him.

Candice's brow furrows. She feels a stab of jealousy.

That's strange.

Jealousy isn't an emotion she's used to feeling. In fact, she tries to feel very few emotions at all. But this rider, this man, has really got under her skin.

And she hates him for it.

CHAPTER THIRTY

HATTIE

Having got Daniel's horses skipped out and hayed, and The Rogue and Pink Fizz walked out to stretch their legs, Hattie heads out of the stables towards the shopping village. As she moves out of the backstage area into the public walkway, her phone vibrates in her pocket. Pulling it out, she smiles as she sees the name on the screen.

Hattie accepts the call. 'Hey there.'

'How are you doing?' asks Liberty, Hattie's ex-neighbour and best friend. 'I thought I'd check in to see how it's all going.'

'It's good,' says Hattie, as she walks between the trade stands. 'The Rogue and Pink Fizz have been jumping really well and Daniel's enjoying it.'

'And you?'

Hattie stifles a sigh. 'I've been enjoying it too.'

'Then why haven't you told your voice that?' asks Liberty, as direct as always. 'You sound deflated.'

'Yeah,' says Hattie. There's no point in denying it; her friend can always pick up on how she's feeling. 'There's this show jumping horse that's having a rough time from its rider. I was thinking about trying to buy him, but the guy says he's already found a buyer – this awful man who has been banned from competition before for abuse of the horse.'

'That's horrific,' says Liberty.

'I know. I can't bear the thought of it. Arthur reminds me of Mermaid's Gold when she first arrived.'

Liberty lets out a long whistle. 'Then you need to go for it.'

'It's too late,' says Hattie, an air of defeat in her tone.

'Sounds to me like you've given up,' says Liberty. 'That's unlike you.'

'Doug has already said this man can have Arthur. And Doug hates me,' replies Hattie, pausing beside a saddlery stand that has a lovely padded leather headcollar that's big enough to fit Arthur. 'There's not much I can do.'

'I'm sure you'll think of something,' says Liberty. 'You always do.'

'Maybe,' says Hattie, unconvinced. 'Anyway, how are you?'

'Great, thanks,' says Liberty, excitement in her voice. 'I've been working on a new range of candle melts and I think I've just cracked it with the right recipe. There's this rhubarb-and-custard one that's going to totally blow your mind.'

'Fantastic,' says Hattie. Liberty makes the most amazing organic candles and wax melts that she sells through her Etsy shop and at local craft fairs. 'I can't wait for you to show me.'

They make plans to get together the following week when Hattie's back from London and then end the call. As she pushes her phone back into her pocket and continues along the walkway, her attention turns to what Liberty said – that she shouldn't give up on Arthur V.

But what can I do?

Doug really does hate her, and if the horse is already promised to Bill Dartmouth there's no way he'll sell him to her instead. Still, she can't stop worrying about the horse. *She* should be the one to give him a home. She needs to find a way.

Shaking her head, Hattie pulls her thoughts away from Doug

and Arthur, and thinks about the things she needs to find. As usual, the trade stands are heaving with people, so it's difficult to see what's on offer until you're right beside, or inside, them. But she promised to help Wayne get everything he needs to propose to Megan in a unique and unusual way, and there's no way she's going to go back on that pledge.

Starting on the left, Hattie walks along the stands, looking inside each one to scan what they have available. She's managed to wangle them parts in the show's Christmas finale on Sunday afternoon. Luckily, the show will provide most of their costumes, but there are a few finishing touches she'd like to get to make things perfect. Finding what she needs here is a long shot, but before she ventures out into London, she wants to be sure.

It's slow going; the walkways are packed with shoppers all filled with the festive shopping spirit. Hattie navigates around parents buying stocking fillers, young riders excited by the latest sparkly riding wear, and serious competitors looking for tack and equipment bargains. She takes a moment to admire the gorgeous carved rocking horses on one of the stands, and some impressive equestrian art and bronze sculptures on another. Sadly there's no sign of any of the things she needs.

Having reached the far end of the trade stands, Hattie is still empty handed. She loops back around on the other side, checking out the remaining stands, but still has no luck. Arriving back at the entrance, she decides to admit defeat.

That's when she feels the sensation again.

Hattie shivers as the hairs on the back of her neck stand on end.

It feels as if someone is staring at her.

Whipping round, Hattie scans the people milling around her, but no one seems to be looking in her direction. Inside, they're chatting with their friends, or looking at the stuff for sale in the trade stands. But she can feel it: the weirdest sensation of being watched. Again.

Who is it?

Hattie surveys the crowd around her. She remembers how the woman with ice-blonde hair in the VIP area seemed to be staring at her and Daniel the previous evening, but she doesn't spot the woman here now.

It's so strange.

Why would anyone be watching me or following me? It doesn't make sense.

I must just be being paranoid, thinks Hattie, shaking her head.

Pushing thoughts of blonde-haired women from her mind, she strides away from the shopping village and out through the main entrance into the frigid afternoon air.

It's so cold, it's as if she can taste ice on her tongue. Hattie looks up and sees that the sky is thick with cloud. She wonders if it's going to snow.

Zipping up her coat, Hattie raises her hand to flag down a nearby cab and hops inside. She still doesn't know where to find the things she needs, but she knows where she's going to start the hunt.

'Where to, love?' asks the beanie-wearing, fleece jumper-wearing cabbie.

Hattie smiles. 'Oxford Street, please.'

Surely she'll find what she needs there.

CHAPTER THIRTY-ONE

ELLA

Tonight's big class is the Santa Stakes and so far luck has been on her side. Both Eagle's Crest and On-The-Up jumped clear in the first round, and now they're through to the second round along with the other eight horse-and-rider combinations who were clear.

Ella's third to go in the jump-off riding On-The-Up, her less experienced horse. As she keeps the mare moving in the collecting ring, Ella tries to listen to what's happening in the main arena for an indication of how the shortened course of fences is riding. She knows the fences have gone up, and the turns are now much tighter and more technical than in the first round. She hopes she and her horses are up to the job.

'And that's a fast clear round for our first competitor in the Santa Stakes second round, Fernando Alma and La Zanahoria, who've set a cracking time to beat,' announces the commentator. 'Next up, we have Otto Schneider riding MWS GmbH's Salvadoro.'

She watches Fernando and La Zanahoria exit the arena. The show jumper is stroking his horse's neck as he tells her how fast and clever she is in Italian. It makes Ella smile. Then she hears the buzzer in the arena go to instruct Otto to start his round. Ella knows she'll be in the ring very soon.

Nerves flare in her chest.

The steward beckons her across to the arena entrance. Ella nods to show that she's on her way, and turns On-The-Up across the collecting ring to the gate. As she approaches the steward, Ella swallows down the butterflies flapping wildly in her stomach, trying to get a handle on her nerves.

It's okay. You've got this, she tells herself.

She really hopes that she has.

From inside the arena, she hears the knocking of hooves on poles. The audience gasps. Once, and then again.

'And that's the last two down for Otto Schneider and Salvadoro,' says the commentator. 'Next up, we have Ella Cooper riding her own On-The-Up.'

'You can go in now,' says the steward. 'Good luck.'

'Thank you,' says Ella, forcing a smile through her nerves.

She rides through into the international arena, blinking at the sudden brightness of the lights. Otto nods to her as he exits, and then it's just her and On-The-Up with the course of jumps. They're much bigger than the first round, and she feels a twinge of worry that On-The-Up will find them too much. Then she reminds herself what a scopey jumper the mare is, and that although she doesn't have the same mileage at this level as Eagle's Crest, she's always loved the job.

The buzzer goes, indicating they can start their round.

'Come on, girl,' says Ella. 'We've got this.'

On-The-Up sets off at a bouncy canter. Her ears are pricked forward, and her focus is on the jumps. As they turn towards the first fence, Ella feels a sense of calm come over her. There's nothing like jumping to make you be entirely in the moment.

On-The-Up leaps over the first – a wide oxer of orange poles – and canters on to the second – a tall vertical made up of grey planks with turkeys painted on them. She soars over them, giving at least a foot of air between the top plank and her hooves, and then turns tightly to the left, looping back over a double of oxers with Christmas cracker fillers beneath them.

Ella asks the mare to turn sharp right after the double, and they leap over a narrow upright with a huge Christmas pudding filler, and then gallop on towards the last – a huge triple bar with eight-foot-tall inflatable Santas on either side of the fence.

On-The-Up never falters, speeding up and over the triple bar. It's only once she's airborne that she lets out a loud snort at the inflatables.

Ella laughs as they land and gallop through the finish to stop the clock. She strokes the mare's neck. 'Good girl. Well done. You did it.'

'And that's a clear for Ella Cooper and On-The-Up,' says the commentator. 'Putting them into second place at this point in the competition.'

As she exits the arena, Doug Wallingford enters on his bay gelding, Spicetown.

'Good luck,' says Ella, smiling.

Doug says nothing, ignoring her.

'Rude,' mutters Ella, under her breath.

She refuses to let Doug's snotty behaviour take the shine off On-The-Up's clear round. She strokes the mare's neck again.

'Well done,' says the steward at the gate.

'Thanks,' replies Ella, grinning. 'She was such a good girl.'

'Great round,' says Joe, riding over on Pipplemouse, his skewbald gelding. 'How's the course riding?'

'It's okay,' says Ella, riding On-The-Up on a long rein alongside Pipplemouse. 'But the turn to the skinny fence with the Christmas pudding rides tighter than I'd anticipated, and the striding down to the triple bar felt long.'

'That's good to know, thanks,' says Joe. 'I'm in soon.'

'Good luck,' says Ella. 'I've got to switch onto Eagle's Crest now. I'm last to go on him.'

'Good luck to you too,' says Joe. 'Let's see if we can take all the top spots between us.'

Ella laughs. 'That would be the dream.'

~

There's hardly enough time to take On-The-Up back to her stable and collect Eagle's Crest before Ella has to jump again.

The pressure of a quick changeover makes her clumsy, and getting On-The-Up tied up takes longer than it should do. Leaving her tacked up but with a rug over her, Ella mounts Eagle's Crest and they hurry to the warmup area. She barely has time for a quick walk, trot and canter before the steward is calling her name.

Looking across at the entrance to the international arena, Ella sees that Antonio de Luca is already exiting. Damn it. She doesn't even have time for a jump over one of the practice fences.

Trotting across to the steward, she thanks them as they wave her through, and rides Eagle's Crest through the tunnel into the bright lights of the arena.

'And now, last to jump in this exciting second round for the Santa Stakes is Ella Cooper on her second horse of the competition – Eagle's Crest,' says the commentator.

The audience applauds. Then, as the buzzer sounds, a hush falls over the crowd.

Here we go.

Asking Eagle's Crest to pop into canter, Ella steers him down the arena to the start. He feels confident and happy to be back in the international arena, and as they turn towards the first fence, Ella whispers, 'Here we go, boy.'

Eagle's Crest jumps the orange oxer at one and the turkey fence at two with ease, then makes a super tight turn to the left, popping the Christmas cracker double as if it's barely a foot high, before turning incredibly tight back to the right and leaping over the narrow upright with the Christmas pudding filler below it. He's got the triple bar in his sights and Ella finds she hardly needs to guide him as he lengthens his stride and flies over the jump without a second glance at the inflatable Santas on either side.

As they race through the finish, the crowd cheers and applauds. Eagle's Crest gives a little toss of his head, as if to say, 'Yes, cheer me, didn't I jump well.'

Grinning, Ella rubs his neck. 'Clever boy, you were so fast.'

'And that's another sterling round from Ella Cooper, this time with Eagle's Crest, which puts them into second place.'

Ella can hardly believe her ears. She thought they were fast, but to be second is amazing. She looks up at the electronic timer fixed high above the arena to double check she heard the commentator correctly.

She did. Her position in the class is displayed clearly on the screen. They've got second.

Leaning forward as she brings Eagle's Crest back to a walk, she releases her reins and strokes the gelding's neck with both hands. 'You were amazing,' she tells him. 'So clever.'

As she rides out of the arena, several of the riders come over to congratulate her. She smiles her thanks to them but she can't hang around. The prize-giving will happen very soon, and as the prizes go to tenth she'll need to ride Eagle's Crest and lead On-The-Up into the arena to collect their rosettes.

~

She's almost late – it's not easy co-ordinating two horses on a tight timeframe – and Ella still hasn't spoken to Joe before she's ushered into the international arena for the prize-giving.

The steward asks her to line up alongside Fernando Alma and his little speedster, La Zanahoria, who've won the class, and Doug Wallingford and his bay gelding, Spicetown, who's in third.

'Congratulations,' says Fernando, giving her a warm smile.

'Thank you so much,' gushes Ella, grinning. 'And huge congrats to you.'

'I am blessed with a wonderful horse,' replies Fernando.

Me too, thinks Ella stroking Eagle's Crest's neck and then leaning across to pat On-The-Up.

'Good work,' says Doug Wallingford, gruffly.

Ella glances at him, and sees that he's kind of smiling at her. 'Thanks, you too.'

'You rode well,' Doug says, nodding approvingly. 'Keep it up.'

'Thanks. I'll try,' says Ella, thinking that on this occasion it seems Doug's probably trying to be encouraging rather than patronising.

'And so now to the presentation of the prizes,' says the commentator, as a smartly dressed older couple flanked by a steward carrying a basket of rosettes step out into the arena in front of them. 'Tonight, Lord and Lady Caverstall will be presenting the prizes in reverse order. So, in tenth place we have Otto Schneider riding MWS GmbH's Salvadoro; in ninth is Lucia Mason riding Purple Palace.'

There's a huge cheer from the crowd as Lucia Mason's placing is announced and the smartly dressed couple step forward to present her with her rosette. Ella smiles. Although relatively new to top level, Lucia has over a million social media followers, and her #showjumpinghacks on Instagram are hugely popular with aspiring show jumpers. She's even used a few of them herself.

'In eighth we have Joe Broughton and Pipplemouse, then in seventh Fernando Alma and Cookiesweet, in sixth Gavin Ledbury on Captain Fury, and then Aimee Eastford and Zippy Fantastic in fifth.' The commentator pauses to draw breath. 'Our top four were our only clears in the second round of the competition.'

Ella had been wondering why Joe hadn't been higher up the order. Pipplemouse is usually very fast, but they must have had a rare fence down this time. She strokes Eagle's Crest and then

On-The-Up; the fact both her horses jumped clear over a track that caused trouble for so many experienced top-level competitors is amazing.

'So in fourth we have the first of Ella Cooper's rides – On-The-Up.'

'Congratulations,' says Lord Caverstall, resplendent in a navy suit and brown brogues as he shakes her hand.

Lady Caverstall, in a beautiful emerald-green ballgown, attaches the fourth-place rosette to On-The-Up's bridle. 'Well done.'

'Thank you so much,' says Ella, grinning.

As they move to Doug Wallingford to present him with his third prize, Ella glances down the lineup to Joe, hoping to catch his eye. But Joe is staring forward, his expression hard to read.

'And now to second place,' says the commentator, his voice breaking into Ella's thoughts, 'where we have Ella Cooper on her second ride of the class, Eagle's Crest.'

As Lord and Lady Caverstall congratulate her again, and the blue rosette for second place is attached to Eagle's Crest's bridle, Ella feels as if she might burst with pride. As she strokes the gelding's neck and thanks the Caverstalls, she can barely believe this is happening.

The rest of the prize-giving ceremony passes in a dream, although Ella is woken up fast by having to try and contain the excitement of both On-The-Up and Eagle's Crest as they complete a lap of honour behind Fernando Alma and La Zanahoria to the tune of Lady Gaga's 'Poker Face'. She's relieved when they can exit into the collecting ring to allow Fernando his solo victory lap under the spotlight.

Back outside the arena, Ella looks for Joe but she can't see any sign of him or Pipplemouse. She frowns. He only left the arena a few seconds before her; how can he have gone already? And why didn't he wait for her? Every other person at the prize-giving has congratulated her, and her them, with the exception of Joe. Yet he's the person who means the most to her.

She scans the space again, but Joe definitely isn't here. Instead, there are eight children and their Shetland ponies scurrying around the warmup area getting ready for the next race in the Shetland Pony Grand National.

Confused, Ella dismounts Eagle's Crest, runs up her stirrups and loosens the gelding's girth. Taking the reins over the gelding's head, she leads him and On-The-Up back towards the stables.

~

It takes a while to get both horses settled, brushed off and rugged up, and then fix their beds and restuff their haynets. Ella takes her time, pleased that she doesn't have a second class to jump in tonight. She's just about to go and mix up the horses' feeds when she sees Joe riding along the passageway between the stables on Truckle Bay.

Bolting On-The-Up's stable door, Ella turns towards Joe and smiles. 'Hey.'

He looks at her, his expression clouding.

'Well done tonight,' Ella says, feeling rather wrong-footed. She's never seen Joe look so sour.

'Yeah,' says Joe, dismissively. 'Look, I can't chat. I have to go and warm up.'

'No problem,' says Ella. 'We could always grab a...'

She lets her words trail off as Joe rides past, his gaze fixed straight ahead and his expression impassive. What's going on? She doesn't understand. Before the class, Joe was warm and kind and funny. Now he seems distant, angry even. She understands that he might be annoyed with himself if he had a pole down, but that's no reason to take it out on her.

As she watches him ride away down the passageway towards

the international arena, there's only one reason Ella can think of that's caused such a big change in the way he behaves towards her – the fact that she beat him in the Santa Stakes.

Surely he can't be that bad a loser?

But it seems like he is.

Ella shakes her head, disappointed. She'd really thought Joe was different, but it seems as if deep down he's just like Henry – he can't stand a woman placing higher than him. It's pathetic. Sighing, she can't help but feel gutted.

'Hello, honey.'

Ella spins around at the sound of the familiar voice. 'Mum?'

'We can't let our little girl stay here all week on her own, can we?' says Ella's dad. 'We've come to cheer you on in the World Cup qualifier tomorrow.'

Ella rushes to her parents and flings her arms around them, her sadness at Joe's behaviour eclipsed by her joy at her parents' arrival.

'Thank you,' says Ella, beaming. 'This is the best surprise ever.'

SUNDAY

CHAPTER THIRTY-TWO

JOE

Joe feels like a dick.

He never meant to take out his bad mood on Ella. The four faults he got in the Santa Stakes jump off were his fault, not hers, and now he's totally gone and blown things.

Joe sighs. He should've seen this coming. He knows what he's like. Striving for perfection has been a part of him ever since he was a little kid. And that, combined with the expectation put on his shoulders by the show jumping community and the media – the universal belief that he should be a world-class rider, that it's in his blood – and the fact that he doesn't want, that he can't, tarnish the memory of his dad by letting him down, has made Joe increasingly self-critical.

When he makes a mistake, he retreats into himself. It's like a dark cloud descends on him and all he can see is his failure. He's got a bit better at lifting himself out of the funk, but when things happen like last night in the Santa Stakes – a rookie error in over-correcting Pipplemouse's forward stride that resulted in the skewbald gelding not reaching the fence in the right spot and knocking the top pole down for four faults – he takes it very much to heart.

That's why he was curt and distracted with Ella when she'd tried to speak with him. It's why he cut her off when she'd been about to ask him to get together later that evening. He's not good company when the funk gets to him. She's better off keeping her distance when he's in that kind of mood. But now he realises he should have told her how he was feeling and why it was better to give last night a miss. To be honest, thinking back now, he's not even sure it was a good idea. He and Ella have a connection. Spending time with her, talking through the round and how he could've ridden, would probably have helped rather than hindered. He wishes that he'd been more open with her now.

As he lies in bed remembering the confused and hurt look on her face as he'd made his flimsy excuse and ridden away, Joe feels awful.

Will she forgive me?

Should she?

He doesn't know, but he has to try and make amends.

Getting out of bed, Joe quickly washes, then pulls on his jeans and a sweatshirt, grabs his puffa jacket and heads out of the hotel to the showground. It's just gone eight o'clock in the morning and the stables are a hive of activity, but Ella isn't with her horses. She's clearly already been here, though – both Eagle's Crest and On-The-Up are contentedly munching on newly filled haynets, and their stables have already been mucked out.

Where is she?

Leaving the stables, Joe heads towards the area where the competitors and grooms staying in their lorries are parked. He walks along the line of horseboxes, trying to think of the best way to apologise. Then he stops. What is he thinking? He can't show up empty-handed, not after how he behaved last night. He needs to bring Ella a peace offering.

I know just the thing.

Turning round, he hurries away from the lorry park.

Twenty minutes later, with two coffees in a holder in one hand and a paper bag containing two bacon butties in the other, all from the café he took Ella to the first time they had breakfast together, Joe returns to the living-in lorry parking area.

Hurrying along the rows of horseboxes, he spots Ella's lorry towards the end of the row up ahead and increases his pace. He nods hello to the people he passes, but he doesn't stop to chat. Ella is important. Apologising to her and admitting he behaved like a dick is his top priority.

He slows as he approaches her horsebox. Anxiety flares inside him. He still doesn't know what to say or how to say it, but he'll start with 'I'm sorry' and go from there.

Taking a breath, he tries to steady his rapidly beating heart, and then knocks on the door of the horsebox's living area and waits.

His heart rate accelerates. His mouth feels dry.

Ella doesn't open the door.

Why isn't she answering? Is she so angry with me that she won't open the door?

Joe knocks on the door again. This time a bit harder and for a little longer. 'Ella, are you in there?'

Again, there's no answer.Putting the coffees and paper bag down on the tarmac, Joe climbs up the steps to the living door. Holding the grip handles at the side of the doorframe, he swings his body to the left and peers into the lorry through the living space window.

It's empty. Ella isn't home.

Dejected, Joe climbs back down the steps and picks up the breakfast items from the ground.

Where is she?

He needs to find her.

Perhaps she's gone to get breakfast, he thinks. It's worth a shot. He doesn't know where she'd have chosen for breakfast – they've always eaten the bacon butties from the café when he's been with her – but there are a few options not too far from here on the showground.

He starts by heading to the food trucks backstage near the stables and the forge, but there's no sign of Ella there, so he continues on, into the public areas of the showground. The Hand & Flower pub doesn't open until later in the morning, but the Riders' Bar on the other side of the collecting ring serves a buffet breakfast until 10 am so he heads in that direction.

That's where he finds her. She's sitting with an older couple at a table in the far corner of the bar. They're chatting animatedly as they tuck into a full English breakfast with toast and coffee. Joe can't see Ella's face as she's sitting with her back to where he's standing just inside the doorway, but he can see the faces of the older couple.

There's something of Ella in both of them. These people have to be her parents. As he watches them talking, and the man, Ella's dad, reaches across the table and gives her arm a squeeze, Joe feels a pang of grief.

He wishes his own dad was here. Dad always knew how to work through a situation. He'd have coached Joe out of his funk last night and would've encouraged him to spend time with Ella.

Leaving her to enjoy her time with her parents, Joe blinks back tears as he rushes out of the Riders' Bar.

God, he misses his dad.

CHAPTER THIRTY-THREE

DANIEL

It's the final class in the eventers vs show jumpers competition. The league scores stand at two wins each going into this class and, as they walk the course, the eventers know that they have to win today in order to win the league – and they really want to win the league.

'So what's our strategy?' asks Fliss, the youngest and least experienced member of the team, as they walk as a group towards the first fence – a large oxer over the Christmas pudding filler.

'How about we have Jonathan and Greta jump first as our pathfinders?' suggests Imy, giving the brown pole over the filler a push to see how secure it is in the cups. 'Then Fliss and myself, and then Fergus and Daniel?'

Daniel nods. He doesn't mind going last, even though if it's down to the wire in terms of faults, the pressure will all be on him. 'Sure.'

'Sounds good,' says Fliss, turning her attention to striding out the related distance between the first fence and number two – a tall skinny vertical whose filler depicts three dancing snowmen.

They continue walking the course, from the vertical at two to a double of oxers with Christmas cracker fillers at three, and then looping back to a grey wall, six long strides to a steeplechase-type jump, and then a tight left-handed turn back to the final combination – a tightly strided treble.

The team stand in front of the first fence of the treble. All three fences are made with big Christmas presents positioned beneath them in shiny red wrapping paper and gold ribbon, with red-and-gold poles above. It's a lot of red and green, and Daniel wonders what the horses will make of it.

'Yuck,' says Fliss, grimacing as she looks at the treble. 'This isn't much fun.'

'We'll need to really get the horses back on their hocks before the turn,' says Fergus, thoughtfully. 'That steeplechase fence is going to encourage them to go long and flat.'

'Very much so,' says Jonathan, with a wry smile, running his hand through his short, curly blond hair. 'Dicky the course designer is certainly showing us his sense of humour today.'

'It'll be okay,' says Imy, firmly. 'We just need to ride it as Fergus said.'

'We're against the clock, though,' says Daniel. 'So we can't take too much time. If we tie in faults, it'll come down to which team had the fastest time.'

'This is true,' says Greta, firmly. 'We must be fast.'

'We'll just have to hope the show jumpers rack up more faults than us, then,' says Imy with a smile. 'We need to beat them.'

'Oh yeah,' says Jonathan.

'Absolutely,' agrees Fergus.

Daniel laughs. 'Let's sock it to them.'

'I'm in,' says Fliss, smiling.

'We can do this.' Greta puts her hand into the middle of the group. 'Eventers on three.'

Jonathan puts his hand on Greta's, Fliss puts hers on his, then Daniel, Imy and Fergus follow suit.

Greta clears her throat. 'One, two, three…'

'Eventers!' they chorus.

A few of the spectators nearby in the grandstand hear them and cheer.

The show jumpers, who are walking the course separately rather than as a team, look over at them, eyebrows raised and amusement on their faces, all except for Doug Wallingford who seems to have a perpetual scowl.

'And at the end of the course walk, we seem to have the eventing team doing some kind of pre-game motivational chant,' says the commentator over the loudspeakers. 'Very interesting. I think we're going to be in for a good competition this morning.'

Things go well at first. Jonathan and Tiktac jump a steady clear, followed by Greta and Westworlder jumping a faster clear. And then Fliss and Dark Matter and Imy on Club Garnett jump steady but solid clears.

The show jumpers are raking in the clears too, with Antonio de Luca, Clara Philips, Fernando Alma, Emma Holmer-Watson and Joe Broughton all going clear in decent times. There's just three horses and riders left to jump – Fergus Bingley and Daniel for the eventers and Doug Wallingford for the show jumpers.

As he rides around the collecting ring, Daniel can feel the pressure mounting. It's too close even for the bookies to call.

'Good luck,' he says to Fergus as he rides Rosalind, his ultra-reliable mare, towards the entrance to the international arena.

Daniel hears the commentator announcing Fergus is the next competitor in the ring, and then tunes out the noise from the arena. He focuses instead on giving The Rogue another couple of jumps over the practice fences. The bay gelding pops them happily, and Daniel brings him back to a walk and gives him a long rein. It's only then that he tunes back into what's happening around them.

Fergus's groom is shaking her head.

What's happened?

'And that's an unlucky four faults for Fergus Bingley and Rosalind,' says the commentator. 'Which means the show jumpers have now moved ahead of the eventers. If the last rider for the show jumpers, Doug Wallingford with Arthur V, goes clear, that means the show jumpers are guaranteed to win the competition today and the league overall.'

Shit.

Daniel watches as a grim-faced Doug and Arthur V head into the arena. The horse doesn't look happy, snatching at the bit and Doug's heavy contact on the reins. In fact, Daniel was surprised to see Doug riding the younger grey horse again today, but apparently he's resting his top horses for the World Cup qualifier this afternoon, and his other younger horse has a bit of heat in its tendon so Doug didn't want to risk jumping them today.

As Doug disappears through the tunnel to the international arena, Daniel knows one thing for sure. Whatever happens in the next few minutes will decide this competition.

CHAPTER THIRTY-FOUR

HATTIE

In the stands, Hattie feels her stomach lurch as Doug Wallingford rides into the arena on Arthur V. The big grey gelding is clearly unhappy, snatching at the reins and shaking his head every few strides, and the cheering of the crowd isn't doing anything to help. Doug looks even more unhappy than his horse; his jaw is set rigid, his mouth in a thin line and a deep frown beneath his hat.

'He's riding that horse again?' says Lady Pat, surprise in her tone. She and Gerald arrived just before the start of the competition to lend some moral support and encouragement to the eventers. Lady Pat is using her opera glasses to get a closer look at Doug's riding.

Hattie nods. 'He wasn't planning to but his other option tweaked their tendon so he's back on poor old Arthur.'

'Interesting,' says Lady Pat, her gaze staying focused on Doug and Arthur. 'Let's see how they do, then. We really need them to have a bit of trouble so our team can win.'

'That's not very sporting,' says Gerald, from the other side of Lady Pat.

'Be that as it may, it's the truth,' replies Lady Pat.

Gerald tuts but says nothing. He lifts his phone, ready to film the round, just as he has with each of the previous competitors.

In the arena, as Doug salutes to the judges, Arthur spooks at one of the large flower arrangements beside the timing equipment for the finish line, taking Doug by surprise. As the grey shoots sideways, Doug loses a stirrup and for a moment it looks as if he might come off, but, as a loud gasp goes up from the audience, he just manages to regain his balance.

The buzzer goes for Doug to start, and Hattie feels her heart rate accelerate as she watches the show jumper put Arthur into canter and move across the arena towards the first fence.

Arthur balloons over the jump – giving the Christmas pudding filler a wide berth.

'Blimey,' says Lady Pat, watching through her opera glasses. 'The horse can certainly jump.'

'Yes,' says Hattie, as she clasps her hands together nervously. 'He can.'

In the arena, Arthur canters on to the skinny vertical with the dancing snowmen filler at two. On the last couple of strides, the grey seems to falter and Doug pushes him on strongly. The gelding leaps high over the jump – clearing the top pole by more than an extra foot. As he lands, Arthur gives a little toss of his head, clearly unhappy with the way Doug pushed him. Doug doesn't seem to notice, or if he does he doesn't care. He keeps pushing the horse on towards fence three – a double of oxers with Christmas cracker fillers beneath them.

Arthur jumps better through the double.

'Nicely done,' says Lady Pat. 'Although Doug is rather chasing the poor fellow.'

Hattie nods. She wonders if the horse will settle now. But then Doug uses a strong rein to turn the gelding back towards number four – a large, grey wall – and the horse throws his head up in protest.

'That was unnecessary,' remarks Lady Pat, looking distinctively unimpressed. 'Doug is too rough; he's pulled the horse right off his rhythm.'

Hattie feels her breath catch in her throat as the grey's hindquarters spin out, and he almost loses his footing. Somehow, though, they make the impossibly tight turn, but they're too close to the fence. Hattie holds her breath and clenches her fists tight.

Amazingly, Arthur manages to get himself into the air and not touch the coping stones on the top of the wall. As they land, Doug kicks the horse on towards the steeplechase-type jump at five. The distance is for six long strides, but Arthur landed short from his mighty leap over the wall, and struggles to make up enough ground. At the last moment, he realises that he's too far off the steeplechase fence and chips in an extra small stride.

Smart boy, thinks Hattie.

The audience gasp.

Gerald lets out a nervous, 'Oh.'

But Arthur again manages to clear the fence, even though it might not be in the best style. Doug seems undeterred by the errors they're making. He yanks the gelding hard to the left, looping him back to the final fences – the short-strided treble.

Lady Pat is shaking her head.

In the arena, Arthur is looking increasingly unhappy. His tail is swishing and he's grinding his teeth against his bit. Hattie feels sick. Poor Arthur; he doesn't deserve this rough treatment from Doug, no horse does.

The treble looms up ahead of Arthur and Doug. The three fences with their large faux Christmas presents wrapped in shiny red paper and tied with gold ribbon, along with the red-and-gold poles above them, glint bright and sparkly in the arena lights.

As he lines up for them, Arthur throws up his head and gives a couple of loud snorts.

Doug spurs the horse on towards the fences.

Arthur's tail swishes faster. He starts putting on the brakes.

Doug smacks his whip onto the gelding's backside. 'Get on.'

Hattie flinches as the whip hits Arthur. She thinks that he's going to refuse at the fence, but then he seems to change his mind. In an almighty effort, the grey gelding leaps over the first part of the treble, but he's too close to clear the top pole and it falls.

The crowd gasp.

Spooked by the error, and by Doug continuing to kick and whip him forward, Arthur fails to get enough height at the next two elements and has the top poles from those fences down too.

'Bloody horse,' says Doug, yanking Arthur sharply in the mouth.

Arthur doesn't appreciate the rough treatment. Letting out a loud squeal, he makes his feelings known by putting in a huge buck. Doug manages to sit it, but Arthur isn't finished.

The grey gelding launches himself forwards and up into the air as if he's aiming for the moon, throwing Doug back in the saddle. Then, as he reaches the highest he can, Arthur adds in a corkscrew twist followed by three huge bucks.

The audience inhale hard.

Doug tries to stay onboard, but the power of the grey horse's buck is too much and the show jumper is catapulted out the front door and headfirst into the flower arrangement by the timing equipment that Arthur had spooked at in the beginning of his round.

With a face full of synthetic sand and faux flowers, a distinctly dishevelled and furious-looking Doug gets to his feet. Arthur takes one look at his rider and spins on his haunches, galloping across the arena and out through the tunnel into the collecting ring.

'Well, good on Arthur,' says Lady Pat, approvingly. 'Doug was riding him like a total thug. There's no place for that kind of behaviour.'

'I'd be surprised if Wallingford doesn't get a suspension for his conduct,' says Gerald, primly, as he taps a message onto his phone. 'No rider should treat their horse like that. It's just not right.'

'Exactly,' says Hattie, feeling sick to her stomach that any horse is treated in such a mean and disrespectful way. 'The sooner Arthur is away from that man the better, but he can't go to Bill Dartmouth, he just can't.'

'Well, I say,' observes the commentator, rather uncharacteristically not seeming to know what to say. 'Yes, well... that's twelve faults for Doug Wallingford and Arthur V. As the fall was incurred after horse and rider had passed through the finish line, they have not been eliminated, but given the faults they've just incurred that may be of little solace to the show jumping team.'

Doug glares up at the commentary box angrily, and for a moment Hattie thinks he's going to shake his fist, or worse, towards the commentator.

Instead, Doug shakes his head and strides out of the arena.

CHAPTER THIRTY-FIVE

DANIEL

It's mayhem in the collecting ring. Arthur V shouldn't have been able to leave the ring the way he did, but the stewards had just opened the gate for Daniel to ride into the arena, and the gelding's speedy exit caught them by surprise.

The Rogue was surprised too when the large grey hurtled out of the tunnel and almost barrelled into him. Luckily, Rogue has always been the friendly type and didn't tell the wild-looking younger horse off. Instead, the grey seemed drawn to Rogue's calm demeanour and, after a couple of laps of the collecting ring, the gelding tucked in beside Rogue, allowing Daniel to take hold of the grey horse's reins and make sure he didn't gallop all the way back to the stables.

'It's okay, boy,' says Daniel, stroking the horse's neck. 'What happened in there?'

The grey is sweating and shaking all over.

'You're okay,' says Daniel, rubbing the horse's neck. 'You're safe.'

Poor chap, thinks Daniel. Whatever happened in the ring has completely freaked the grey gelding out.

'I'm so sorry,' says Pippa, the youngest and newest recruit to

Doug's groom team, rushing over on foot to collect Arthur. 'He didn't crash into you, did he?'

'No, he's fine,' says Daniel, handing Arthur's reins to Pippa. 'What happened in there?'

Pippa grimaces. 'Doug was being heavy-handed and bullish with the whip. He knows Arthur's sensitive, but he doesn't care.' She shakes her head. 'Well, today he pushed Arthur too far and the sweet boy retaliated. It wasn't Arthur's fault; he's a sweet horse – really, he is. But Doug just winds him up and gets frustrated.'

'I saw a bit of that kind of thing the other day,' says Daniel sympathetically. 'Have you tried speaking to Doug about changing tactics?'

Pippa lets out a hollow laugh. 'Oh my God, Doug would chew my ear off if I did that. I'm just the help to him.'

'I'm sorry,' says Daniel. 'Eddie, who works with me, is invaluable in giving me tips and ideas for things to try with the horses. I've really missed his input this week – he's at home looking after the yard and keeping the youngsters in training.'

Pippa gives him a wistful look. 'That's something I can only dream of with Doug.' She shakes her head. 'Anyway, after this show is over I'm going to look for another job. I've had enough. I didn't get into this game to watch a rider bully his horses.'

'Good luck,' says Daniel.

'Thanks,' says Pippa, grimacing. 'I can only imagine how pissed off Doug will be after getting dumped in front of the audience.'

As if on cue, Doug emerges into the collecting ring. When he sees Daniel talking to Pippa, and Arthur standing alongside The Rogue, the show jumper swears under his breath and marches toward them.

'Bloody horse,' snaps Doug, ignoring Daniel and focusing on Pippa. 'Get it out of my sight.'

'Whatever happened in there wasn't Pippa's fault,' says Daniel evenly.

Doug glares up at Daniel on The Rogue. There's still some synthetic sand clumped around his left eyebrow. 'Piss off.'

Daniel spots the steward beckoning him over to the entrance to the arena. He looks down at Doug, fixing him with a steely gaze. 'In fact, from what I've seen over the last few days, I'd say that whatever happened out there in the arena, you brought it on yourself.'

Doug's eyes widen and his lips flap like a fish out of water. 'Don't you bloody well go and—'

'You should treat your horses and your grooms a damn sight better,' says Daniel. Then he turns The Rogue towards the entrance of the arena and rides away, leaving Doug cursing.

CHAPTER THIRTY-SIX

DANIEL

As he rides into the international arena, Daniel can feel the electricity in the air. The Rogue can feel it too and he jigs rather than walks, finding it hard to stay long in halt while Daniel salutes to the judges.

'And last to ride in this thrilling eventers vs show jumpers league competition is Daniel Templeton-Smith riding his own The Rogue,' announces the commentator. 'Daniel needs fewer than eight faults if the eventers are to win the league.'

No pressure then, he thinks. The last few minutes in the collecting ring – catching Arthur and the run-in with Doug – weren't especially conducive to getting himself in the zone for this. But Daniel knows what's expected – his teammates are relying on him – and he's going to do his best to secure the win.

He asks The Rogue to get going and the big bay gelding jumps eagerly into canter, putting in a high-spirited buck for good measure. The audience gasp and then clap as Daniel grins at Rogue's antics and gives the horse a rub on his neck rather than a reprimand.

Now it's time to focus.

They make their way down to the far end of the arena and the first fence with the Christmas pudding filler. The Rogue makes easy work of it and canters on to the narrow vertical without batting an eyelid at its brightly coloured filler of dancing snowmen. Daniel asks the big bay gelding to lengthen his stride into the double of oxers with the Christmas cracker fillers at three, and Rogue responds happily, taking a stride out of the regular pacing and flying easily over the fences.

So far, so good.

The grey wall is next. It looks massive today, but The Rogue isn't daunted. He glides around the turn without changing pace and leaps over the wall, making the six strides to the steeplechase-style fence with ease.

Some people in the crowd start to cheer.

A woman close to the edge of the arena shouts, 'Come on, Daniel.'

The Rogue speeds around the last turn, heading for the final combination.

Daniel fights to stay focused – they still have the troublesome treble to jump. He wants to ask The Rogue to steady but the horse feels confident and on form, and time is everything in today's competition. If they were to have a couple of poles down now, the time would be the deciding factor. So Daniel lets the gelding maintain his speed and rides forward to the fence.

The shiny green-and-gold Christmas presents don't faze The Rogue. He glides over each of the fences without touching a pole.

As they land over the last, the audience goes wild – cheering and applauding. There are even some Pony Clubbers chanting Daniel's name and waving signs with The Rogue's name in red hearts.

'Good boy. Amazing work,' says Daniel, grinning as he rubs The Rogue's neck over and over. 'You can have a whole packet of ginger biscuits for that.'

'And Daniel Templeton-Smith and The Rogue jump clear to secure victory for the eventers,' says the commentator. 'After a neck-and-neck battle over the week, we finally have our winners. Join us at the prize-giving ceremony in just a few minutes.'

As Daniel and The Rogue exit, the arena crew in their red t-shirts charge into the ring to clear the jumps from the space.

The Rogue gives a little snort as the tractor pulling the jump trailer passes him. Daniel strokes the horse's neck. 'Steady.'

'Wasn't he fantastic,' says Hattie, rushing over to meet Daniel and The Rogue as they emerge into the collecting ring. 'He jumped brilliantly, just like the total star he is.'

'He was amazing,' says Daniel, feeling suddenly emotional. 'He pulled out all the stops.'

'Here you go,' says Hattie to The Rogue, feeding the big gelding half a ginger biscuit. 'You were bloody brilliant.'

'Well done, Danny,' says Greta, riding up on Westworlder and giving Daniel a pat on the back. 'We did it.'

'Thanks,' says Daniel. 'We did, didn't we?'

'What a round,' says Fliss, riding alongside them on Dark Matter. 'I can't believe we won.'

'Fair and square,' says Jonathan, halting nearby on Tiktac.

'Absolutely,' agrees Fergus, stopping beside them on Rosalind. 'Great round, Daniel.'

'You did a wonderful job,' says Imy, joining them with Club Garnett.

As Hattie feeds The Rogue another piece of ginger biscuit, Dark Matter cranes her neck towards Hattie, opening her mouth.

Hattie laughs. 'Do you like ginger biscuits too?'

'She loves all food,' says Fliss. 'Although she's never had a ginger biscuit.'

'Here you go then,' says Hattie, feeding the mare a piece of biscuit. 'See what you make of that.'

The mare crunches the biscuit, suspiciously at first, then more enthusiastically as she gets used to the unfamiliar flavour. She open her mouth for more.

Hattie looks at Fliss. 'I guess she likes it.'

'Seems that way,' agrees Fliss, laughing.

The Rogue looks momentarily put out, before Hattie gives him more biscuit and his ears flick forwards again.

'Jolly well done,' says Lady Pat, striding towards the team with Gerald. 'That was a superb piece of riding, Daniel.' She looks around the gathered event riders. 'You should all be very proud. You really showed those show jumpers what you're made of, and beating them on their home turf, so to speak, is very impressive.'

'One show jumper certainly showed a different side to him,' mutters Fliss, frowning. 'I used to idolise Doug Wallingford when I was a kid.'

'Yes, I saw that,' says Lady Pat, disappointment in her tone. 'In fact, we're on our way to the show manager's office now to lodge a formal complaint. That sort of behaviour simply mustn't be tolerated.'

'Please add my name to the complaint,' says Hattie.

'And mine,' adds Daniel. 'It's not the first time Doug's taken his anger out on that horse.'

The other eventers nod.

'Us too,' says Greta, speaking for the group. 'Please.'

'Very good.' Lady Pat nods. 'We will. Now, we must hurry or we won't be back to see your prize-giving.'

As Gerald and Lady Pat stride off to the show manager's office, Hattie feeds all of the horses a piece of ginger biscuit. Daniel hopes Lady Pat's complaint is upheld. There should be no place for that kind of behaviour in sport, or in anything. The welfare and safety of the horses must always come first. Otherwise, what's the point?

CHAPTER THIRTY-SEVEN

DANIEL

As they ride into the international arena for the last time, Daniel feels a lump in his throat as the emotion of the moment hits home. After all the stress and anxiety of the previous year when The Rogue was injured and Daniel was beholden to Lexi Marchfield-Wright in so many ways, this year has been amazing: winning Badminton, Hattie moving in, and now topping off the year with this team win at London International Horse Show. Well, Daniel can't imagine things could get much better than this.

The arena is cleared of jumps, the arena crew having worked at lightning-fast speed as usual, and at the far end, the now-familiar huge flower arrangements in massive urn-type pots have been positioned as markers for the horses and riders to line up between them. The audience is clapping and cheering. Across in the riders' stand, Daniel spots Hattie sitting with Lady Pat, Gerald and Megan. Hattie waves and blows a kiss as their eyes meet. Daniel grins. Upbeat music is being played over the speakers. It's a real party atmosphere.

As the eventers line up on the left side, Greta leads the group, followed by Fliss, Jonathan, Imy and Fergus, with Daniel and The

Rogue completing the team. The show jumpers line up to Daniel's right, in second place. But something's different. They only have five team members in the arena, not six.

That's when Daniel realises Doug Wallingford is missing.

'Where's Doug?' asks Daniel, turning to Joe Broughton, who is lined up to his right.

Joe grimaces. 'After what he did earlier, he's been suspended pending investigation and banned from competing for the rest of the show.'

'Was it because of the complaints made?' replies Daniel.

Joe shakes his head. 'It was almost immediate from what I've heard.'

'Good,' says Daniel, nodding to himself.

'Congratulations on the win by the way.' Joe holds out his hand. 'You guys beat us fair and square.'

Laughing, Daniel shakes the show jumper's hand. 'It was pretty down to the wire.'

'The best competitions always are,' says Joe, smiling. 'That horse of yours has a great jump. If you ever tire of eventing you could come and join us show jumpers.'

'I'd miss the cross-country too much.'

'That's a shame,' says Joe, with a rueful shrug. 'But never say never.'

'And now it's time for the prize-giving for this year's eventers vs show jumpers league competition,' says the commentator. 'It was a close run, neck-and-neck battle this year, with everything resting on the final class, but in the end the eventers emerged victorious. Presenting the prizes is one of our sponsors, Arnold T. Gladstone, who is accompanied by his wife, Candice Gladstone.'

At the arena's edge, a door opens and an older gentleman in a perfectly tailored black suit and bow tie, his salt-and-pepper hair cropped short, walks into the arena with the aid of a black cane. Behind him, a woman with long, ice-blonde hair who's wearing a fitted emerald green dress and impossibly high heels for walking on synthetic sand, follows from the side of the arena.

Daniel's eyes widen.

It's the woman from the VIP section who was staring at me and Hattie earlier in the week. There's something oddly familiar about her.

The couple, accompanied by two stewards carrying baskets of rosettes, make their way across the arena to Greta. Daniel tries not to stare, but no matter how hard he thinks about it, he can't work out how he could have met Candice Gladstone before.

'Firstly, the winners' rosettes will be presented to the eventing team,' says the commentator as Arnold T. Gladstone and Candice Gladstone reach Greta. 'The victorious team are led by Greta Wolfe riding Westworlder, next in line is Fliss Moreton on Dark Matter, Jonathan Scott riding Tiktac, Imy Palmer-Drew on Club Garnett, Fergus Bingley on Rosalind, and Daniel Templeton-Smith with The Rogue.'

The Gladstones move along the line-up, presenting each rider with their rosette and shaking their hand. Daniel feels increasingly anxious as they get closer to him, but he has no idea why. His nerves seem to transmit to The Rogue, who uncharacteristically finds it difficult to stay halted, side-stepping to the right as the Gladstones approach.

Arnold T. Gladstone reaches up towards Daniel, his hand outstretched. His American accent is strong as he says, 'Great job out there.'

'Thank you,' says Daniel, shaking the sponsor's hand. Arnold T. Gladstone seems friendly enough, and Daniel's certain he's never met him before, but still the adrenaline fizzing in his body intensifies.

As Arnold moves on to start presenting the second placed rosettes to Joe Broughton and the show jumpers, his wife, Candice, moves closer to Daniel. Skirting around the front end of The Rogue, she holds out a red first-place rosette and a bigger, green-and-gold rosette with 'EVENTERS VS SHOW JUMPERS

LEAGUE CHAMPION' embossed along one of the ribbons. 'Congratulations.'

As Daniel leans forward and takes the rosettes, The Rogue's ears flick back. He turns his head towards the woman, snapping his teeth. She leaps back in shock.

'What are you doing?' says Daniel to the gelding. He looks at Candice Gladstone. 'I'm so sorry, he's never done that before.'

'I guess he doesn't like me.' She gives a prim shake of her head. 'That's okay.'

As their eyes meet, Daniel feels a jolt of familiarity. His face flushes. The adrenaline inside him surges, and he fights the urge to recoil from this woman.

'Have we met before?' he asks, trying to keep his voice steady.

Candice smiles but shakes her head again. 'I'm sure I'd remember if we had.'

As she continues on along the lineup of show jumpers with her husband, Daniel's anxiety and adrenaline start to ease. Still, he can't shake the feeling that he *has* met Candice Gladstone before, and that it wasn't a good experience.

He just wishes he could remember.

CHAPTER THIRTY-EIGHT

HATTIE

As she's leaving the rider's seating area, Hattie runs straight into Doug.

The show jumper scowls, his face turning red as he sees her. 'You bloody screwed me, you know that, right?'

Hattie frowns. 'I've done nothing to you.'

'Yeah, yeah, it had to be you and your pony-patting friends, spreading bullshit lies about me and how I ride my horses,' Doug rants, his voice rising in volume and drawing the attention of people around them. 'Well congratulations, you've not only got me banned from competing in the World Cup qualifier, so my owners are having a go at me, you've also screwed up the sale of Arthur to Bill Dartmouth – the bastard's more than halved his offer.'

What the hell is he going on about?

Hattie frowns. 'How do you think I—'

'It was you that posted the video on social media, wasn't it?' he shouts, his finger stabbing towards Hattie's face. 'Did it make you feel important and clever? Sharing a video of me getting bucked off to make me look like an idiot? Your bloody pony-patting brigade are trying to get me cancelled.'

'I didn't take any video of you,' says Hattie firmly, standing her ground. 'But it was *you* who made you look like an idiot. You did that all by yourself.'

'You little bitch, you know it was Lady Patricia's assistant who did it,' spits Doug, stepping closer to Hattie. He towers over her menacingly.

'Gerald?' says Hattie, confused. She doesn't think Gerald even knows what social media is, let alone has any social accounts set up. But then she remembers him tapping away on his phone just after taking the video of Doug and Arthur, and how determined both he and Lady Pat had been that Doug should be held accountable for his actions.

'Yes, him,' says Doug. 'He… You screwed me over and…'

Abruptly he stops talking, seemingly just having become aware that they're being stared at by the people leaving the riders' stand and those gathered in the walkway.

Perhaps he's worried about being filmed again?

Hattie feels fury building inside her. She's had enough of Doug's self-important, entitled bullshit. She looks at him with disgust. 'There's no excuse for the way you treated Arthur, and no place for that sort of behaviour in our sport. You're a disgrace, and I'm glad you've been suspended. If you have any sense, you'll think long and hard about what you did and make a decision to change.'

Doug curses under his breath.

Hattie steps around him to leave.

'Oh, and by the way,' says Hattie, turning back around to face him. 'My offer still stands. I'll buy Arthur from you. I'm happy to match whatever price you agreed with Bill Dartmouth.'

'You couldn't afford it,' scoffs Doug, dismissively.

Hattie narrows her eyes. 'Believe me, I can.'

Leaving Doug open mouthed, she strides away from the stands and across the walkway towards the collecting ring entrance.

Her heart's pounding, and she's not sorry for telling Doug a few home truths, but as she walks away, a sadness grows inside her. She just wants to get Arthur safely away from him, and now that seems even more impossible than ever.

CHAPTER THIRTY-NINE

WAYNE

The nerves are getting worse. He'd been too busy in the show forge for most of the morning to think about what's planned for later, but now his shift is over and he and Megan are having lunch at the back of the forge, the fluttering feeling in his chest is getting stronger.

In just a few hours, it'll be time for the proposal and there's still loads to do. Hattie did a great job in finding most of the props he's going to need, but there are still some major logistical issues to overcome and Wayne has no idea how to make them happen.

Still, he smiles and nods as Megan talks about the drama in the eventers vs show jumpers competition this morning, and hopes she can't tell that he's only half listening.

'...so Doug Wallingford has been suspended,' says Megan. 'Which is totally right. You should have seen how he treated his poor horse – so rough.'

'That's awful,' agrees Wayne, taking the last bite of his sandwich.

'It really is.' Megan shakes her head. 'And then Doug accosted Hattie as she was leaving the rider's stand and he had a right go at her, accusing her of filming his fall and putting it online among other things. Don't worry, though, she put him straight and gave him what for.'

'Good,' says Wayne.

Megan finishes the last of her sandwich and takes a sip of fruit juice. 'How were things in here?'

'Yeah, good – pretty busy. I just need to tidy up and then I'm done. That's my last shift finished.'

'The week has gone so fast, hasn't it?' says Megan. 'I know I've been off on some days working, but it seems like we only just got here.'

'It does.' Wayne's almost sad it's over as the show has been a lot of fun, but he's missing home and his animals, so it'll be good to get back to Leightonshire.

'Do you fancy a mooch around the trade stands?' asks Megan, tilting her head to the side. 'We might get some bargains as the show's almost over.'

Wayne shakes his head. 'I should really head back to the hotel. I stink of smoke and could do with a quick shower before we watch the World Cup qualifier.'

I also need to fetch the props and sort the logistics.

'Actually,' says Megan, her voice becoming a little breathy. 'I have a fun idea...'

With Wayne watching, she walks over to the door to the forge and closes it. With an impish smile, she turns the key to lock it, then pulls her jumper over her head and steps out of her boots and jeans, revealing her sexy black lace lingerie beneath.

'Jesus,' says Wayne, already feeling himself hardening.

Megan moves across the space to the anvil and bends over, wiggling her arse at him. 'Want to play?'

Wayne doesn't need asking twice. Pulling off his plaid shirt, he starts undoing his farrier chaps.

'Jeans off, baby,' says Megan, looking over her shoulder seductively. 'But leave your chaps on.'

'Is this some kind of fantasy of yours?' asks Wayne, as he removes his jeans.

'Oh yes,' says Megan. 'Ever since I saw the photo of you in the "Rural Pleasures" calendar.'

Wayne smiles. Last year, he'd posed in his forge, naked aside from his chaps, with just an anvil covering his modesty, as 'Mr March' in a charity calendar titled 'Rural Pleasures'. It was a massive success, earning a lot of money for the charity and making Wayne a bit of a local celebrity to boot. They've shot more pictures for the new calendar, which is due to go on sale next week; if anything, the photo they've chosen of Wayne leaves even less to the imagination.

Kicking off his jeans, he hurries across the forge to Megan. He kisses her neck, inhaling the familiar, sexy scent of her, and slides his hands over her breasts, down her belly and between her legs. She moans, and he can barely hold back.

'I want you,' she murmurs.

Turning Megan around to face him, Wayne kisses her, then picks her up and enters her. Megan closes her eyes and tilts her head back as he fills her.

Damn, she feels so good.

CHAPTER FORTY

ELLA

This is it, the World Cup qualifier. Ella takes a deep breath as she waits for the steward's signal to enter the international arena. She's the last competitor to jump in the first round, and the word from the other competitors is that the course is riding tough. There have only been four clear rounds so far, including one from Joe and Truckle Bay.

I don't want to think about Joe right now.

Ella strokes Eagle's Crest's chestnut neck. He was her first horse and he's taught her everything. She still can't quite believe that they've made it through the ranks together from jumping in the Pony Club to competing here in their first World Cup qualifier. Eagle's Crest is sixteen now, but feels as good as he always has. Whatever happens in the next few minutes, she couldn't be more proud of him. 'We've got this, boy.'

'In you go then,' says the steward, her words breaking into Ella's thoughts. The blonde lady in the blue tweed coat gives Ella a smile, as if realising how nervous she's feeling, and adds, 'Good luck.'

'Thank you,' says Ella, returning the steward's smile, then asking Eagle's Crest to walk into the tunnel.

Here we go.

They pass through the tunnel between the grandstands and emerge into the bright lights of the international arena and the applause of the audience. The stands are packed with people. No seat is empty.

'And last to jump in this first round of the World Cup qualifier is Ella Cooper riding her own Eagle's Crest,' says the commentator as the buzzer sounds.

Ella asks Eagle's Crest to canter, and they travel down the arena towards the first fence. Ella's heart is pounding in her chest. Adrenaline fizzes through her body.

The audience falls silent. Now it feels like just the pair of them and the fences.

They make a good jump over the green-and-white oxer at number one and continue on to the vertical at two. The dog-leg turn has caught out quite a few riders but Eagle's Crest, responsive as ever, makes it feel smooth and clears the upright of white poles easily before they make a right-handed turn to the pink-and-yellow fence at three.

'Steady,' cautions Ella.

Eagle's Crest makes a big jump over three and canters on towards the treble. Ella asks him again to steady and he does, shortening his stride and popping neatly through the tightly-strided vertical to vertical to oxer combination.

There are whispers in the grandstands. Will Ella and Eagle's Crest go clear?

Ella's wondering the same thing. Hoping they will. Really hoping.

They loop around the end of the arena and pop through the blue-and-white double, then make the related distance to the water tray with yellow poles above it, and then they're into the final turn towards the last fence – a vertical with post box-shaped jump-stands holding red poles. They meet the jump on the perfect stride and Eagle's Crest soars into the air. Ella holds her breath and for a moment it feels as if time stops.

Then they land.

They're clear. They've done it.

'Good boy, good boy,' cries Ella, patting Eagle's Crest's neck over and over.

The audience claps and cheers.

'And that's a very solid performance from newcomer Ella Cooper and Eagle's Crest in their first World Cup qualifier, with their clear round putting them forward to the jump off,' says the commentator.

As they head out of the tunnel into the collecting ring, Ella's parents rush out of the stands to congratulate her. Ella dismounts and runs Eagle's Crest's stirrups up and loosens his girth before hugging her parents in a three-way hug.

'That was amazing,' says her mum.

'You smashed it,' her dad tells her, the emotion clear in his voice.

Over her mum's shoulder, Ella sees Joe walking towards them across the collecting ring. She turns away, unable to face speaking to him right now. She needs to stay focused on the competition, not get distracted by a man.

'Wow, a clear round on that old donkey? I suppose I should say well done,' says a sneery male voice from behind her.

Ella freezes. She knows that voice.

What the hell is he doing here?

Whipping round, she finds herself face to face with her ex. 'Henry.'

'I saw those pictures on social media,' says Henry, gesturing towards her with his good arm, the one that isn't in a sling to limit the movement of his injured shoulder. His otherwise handsome face is hardened by jealousy. His piercing pale-blue eyes are full of contempt. 'Had to come and see if it was really true.'

Ella frowns. 'I don't know what you're—'

'You kissing that.' He nods dismissively towards Joe, who's standing a few metres away.

'So what?' says Ella, tilting her chin up defiantly. 'We broke up, Henry. I can do whatever the hell I want.'

'And what if I don't like it?' throws back Henry, puffing out his chest. 'What then, huh?'

Ella turns back to her parents. Handing Eagle's Crest's reins to her mum, she says, 'Would you both walk him round so he doesn't get cold?'

'Of course, love,' says her dad, throwing a woollen rug over the gelding's back. 'We'll look after him.'

'Will you be okay?' asks her mum.

Ella feels sick. Her heart's beating at a hundred miles an hour, but she nods. She has to end this, once and for all. 'Yes, I'll be with you in a minute.'

'A minute – is that all of your time you're willing to give me?' says Henry. 'What happened to forever?'

Ella turns back to face him. 'I never said forever, Henry,' she replies, her tone firm. 'And you were the one who cheated on me, multiple times, so don't try and act the victim here. We're over. Done. And we're *never* getting back together. You need to get that into your head. Whatever you do and whatever you say, it makes no difference.'

Henry glares at her. His cheeks reddening. 'And what if I—'

'If you don't listen, I'll do what I told you I would. I'll go to the police. You've been cyber stalking and harassing me for months, Henry, and I'm not taking it anymore. I've got the proof and I *will* press charges. Also, if you did share the naked pictures of me, I'll have you charged for revenge porn too.'

Henry steps closer to Ella. There's fury in his expression, and even with his arm in a sling he still manages to seem menacing. 'You bloody little —'

'Leave her alone,' says Joe, rushing over and standing between

Henry and Ella. 'You heard what she said; you're not wanted here.'

'And here's lover boy,' sneers Henry. 'Think you're some kind of knight in shining armour, do you? Pathetic!' He leans closer, his face just inches from Joe's. 'Stay away from my girl.'

Ella clenches her fists. 'I'm not your—'

'She's not your girl. You broke up,' says Joe, standing his ground. 'And she'd like you to step away.'

'Just because we broke up, it doesn't mean *you* can have her,' shouts Henry, moving away from Ella and giving Joe a shove with his good arm. 'You jumped-up little prick.'

Joe stumbles backwards.

'Nothing to say for yourself now?' mocks Henry. 'You're pathetic. Maybe you two do deserve each other.' He shrugs, glancing at Ella like she's dirt on his boot. 'Yeah, have her, I'm done with her. She was a crap lay anyway.'

'You bastard,' says Ella, disgust in her tone. 'There's no low you won't sink to, is there? You're talking about me like I'm some kind of possession to have or not have. Well I'm not *anyone's*. I'm my own person. Neither of you own me.'

Henry looks at Joe and laughs. 'See? She doesn't want you, Loverboy, so—'

Joe launches himself at Henry. He's so quick, Henry doesn't have time to defend himself before Joe smacks his fist into his face, then uses his other hand to land a powerful blow into his stomach.

Ella winces. Other competitors and their grooms stop what they're doing to watch the brawl.

This is so embarrassing.

Cursing, Henry falls backwards, landing on his arse on the collecting ring synthetic sand. He clutches at his shoulder, clearly in pain. 'You fucker.'

'No,' says Joe calmly as he looks down at Henry. '*You're* the fucker. Stay away from Ella, and stay away from me.'

'Joe Broughton?' calls the collecting ring steward from the entrance to the international arena. She eyes Joe with a highly disapproving expression. 'You're first to jump in the second round. This is your two-minute warning.'

Joe steps away from Henry, who's still lying on the ground, and turns towards Ella. He opens his mouth to say something, but then stops as their eyes meet.

Ella glares back at him, emotions ricochetting through her.

She sees Joe's face fall and knows that it's because of her expression. But although how she's feeling isn't entirely Joe's fault, she can't bring herself to say anything. She's so furious that Henry came here and made a scene, distracting her from the World Cup qualifier, and she's angry at Joe for stepping in when she was handling Henry just fine.

She didn't want a man to come and save her. She can do that for herself.

CHAPTER FORTY-ONE

JOE

The adrenaline from the fight is still pulsing through Joe as he mounts Truckle Bay, but that's not what's distracting him the most; it's the look on Ella's face – the disappointment and, maybe, disgust – at what he's done. He can't get the image out of his head.

I've let her down.

He's not a fighter and never has been. He hates violence, always has done. Today was the first punch he's ever thrown. He exhales hard.

What was I thinking?

He's blown things with Ella even more now, even worse than he did last night. Joe wonders if there's any way he can come back from this and make it up to her. He really hopes it's possible, but he's not sure it is.

And now he has to jump the second round of the qualifier.

Shit.

The steward, although clearly disapproving of the fight, is kind to him and lets him stretch his two minutes to five, giving him and Truckle Bay the chance for a quick loosener and a pop over a practice fence. But even so, as he rides into the international arena, Joe feels less than adequately prepared.

There's not one spare seat in the grandstands. As the pair of them trot into the arena, the crowd claps. Joe hears people shouting his name and Truck's, and there are more than a few 'I heart Joe' banners being waved. He's pleased for the support, but he tries not to let it distract him from the job in hand. He needs to concentrate and get his head in the game, but although he's trying, it's proving far harder than usual.

After saluting to the judges, Joe touches his bay gelding's neck and says, 'I'm sorry, Truck. I hope I don't let you down.'

The horse jigs into canter as if to say, 'Buck up, Joe, let's get on with this.'

Joe smiles, Truck's reaction lifting his spirits as always. 'Okay, let's do this.'

The course has been shortened from the first round and there are just six jumping efforts now, but the course designer has made the route extra twisty. The only opportunity to save time is by cutting the corners more than the rest of the competitors and to keep on motoring around the turns. It's a risky strategy but one that often suits Truck. Joe hopes it works today.

As they canter down towards the start of the course, the audience's applause fades and an expectant silence falls over the grandstands. This competition is the big one – the one they've all come to see – and they want to be wowed.

Joe and Truckle Bay accelerate through the start markers to the first fence, the green-and-white oxer. It's higher and wider now. Truck clears it easily and speeds on through the dog leg to the white vertical at two, but Joe lets the horse get too fast, and his stride becomes a little flat.

Joe realises his mistake too late, and as the big gelding reaches the fence, Joe fears the horse won't be able to lift his front end up high enough to clear the maximum-height top pole. But somehow Truck does, powering over the vertical and turning lightning-fast around the corner to loop back to the second part of the blue-and-white double, a large oxer.

They jump it on the angle, which makes the turn to the water tray with yellow poles easier, and they leap that on the angle too. They're almost home – just the final fence to jump.

As they land over the water tray, Joe asks Truck to turn and the bay horse responds. In the stands, the crowd is starting to cheer them on, unable to contain their excitement.

Truckle Bay completes the turn and takes two strides to meet the final fence – the red-poled vertical with post box-shaped jump-stands – on the perfect stride. He jumps the fence with inches to spare and they gallop through the finish line, stopping the clock.

'And that's a clear round from Joe Broughton and Truckle Bay,' says the commentator, 'who have set a very quick time for the other competitors to try and beat.'

Joe gives Truck a long rein and rubs the horse's neck. 'Good boy, great work.'

Truck marches jauntily towards the exit, clearly pleased with himself.

Joe smiles, and for a moment he feels happy, lighter. Then he remembers how he's upset Ella and caused a scene with Henry, and the weight of his own mistakes crushes down on him again.

I have to make things right.

CHAPTER FORTY-TWO

ELLA

She's last to jump.

As Ella rides Eagle's Crest into the international arena, she feels her stomach flip and a surge of adrenaline pulse through her body. As the commentator announces them, the audience in the packed-out grandstands applauds. It's like nothing she's experienced before. The atmosphere feels electric. Ella still can't believe she's actually here, competing in the World Cup qualifier jump off. It's literally a dream come true. She refuses to let Henry ruin this for her. He's not worth it. He never was.

She glances up into the riders' section of the stands and sees her mum and dad sitting in the first row. Her dad gives her a smile and her mum raises her hand in a wave.

It's so good to have them here.

Ella salutes to the judges and as the buzzer goes, telling her to start her round, she takes a long breath in to steady her nerves.

She shortens her reins and leans forward, saying to Eagle's Crest, 'Let's have fun.'

The chestnut gelding blows out, as if to reply, 'Yes, please.'

Ella asks him for canter, and they travel down to the bottom of the arena towards the start. Eagle's Crest's canter is strong and purposeful. He loves to jump, Ella knows they need to be fast and she has to trust him if they're going to try for a spot in the top placings. Joe and Truckle Bay are still in the lead with the fastest clear round, but she doesn't want to think about Joe right now. She can't.

Focus.

I have to focus on the course. On Eagle's Crest.

The gelding gives a little shake of his head as if to say, 'Keep your head in the game.'

'I will,' whispers Ella. 'I promise.'

They canter through the start line towards the first fence. It's bigger than in the first round, but Eagle's Crest leaps the green-and-white oxer like it's easy, and continues on smoothly through the dog-leg turn to the white vertical at two.

They get a little close to it, and Ella holds her breath as Eagle's Crest takes off, willing him to clear the fence. He makes a huge jump over it, not touching the poles, and as he lands, Ella asks him to turn tightly back to the large oxer that had been the second part of the double in the first round.

As they're landing over the oxer, Ella asks the chestnut gelding for another tight turn, looping back to the water tray. Eagle's Crest keeps motoring around the turn and makes a good jump over the water tray and yellow poles.

In the grandstands, the audience is still silent. Watching.

We must be in with a chance.

Ella knows everything will depend on this last turn and the last fence. There's a way to cut a few extras seconds off the clock by taking the inside track between a large flower arrangement and the vertical with the post box jump-stands with the red poles. The only people who've tried it have had the last jump down, but their times were faster than those who've gone clear.

It's time to make a decision.

As they land over the water tray, Ella asks Eagle's Crest for the tighter option. The gelding is quick to respond; light on his feet, as always, he whizzes around the turn. They'll have to jump the final fence on an angle. They're a little bit too far off but there are no more strides left.

Eagle's Crest leaps into the air.

Ella holds her breath, willing the gelding upwards.

They fly over the fence and land on the other side, galloping through the finish.

The audience remains silent. Ella strokes Eagle's Crest's neck, and looks behind her to check if the fence stayed up.

The crowd starts to cheer.

Ella looks up at the scoreboard.

Is that right?

Her stomach somersaults. She can't believe it.

'And that's a clear round for Ella Cooper and Eagle's Crest,' says the commentator, his plummy voice laced with excitement. 'And the fastest time of the day, winning them this World Cup qualifier.'

Ella punches the air and throws her arms around Eagle's Crest's neck.

'We did it,' she tells the gelding. 'We actually did it.'

All around them, the audience is going wild. Eagle's Crest prances, as if thrilled to be getting the accolades he deserves.

As the arena crew rush into the arena to remove the jumps, Ella walks Eagle's Crest back towards the exit. She spots her parents in the stand, clapping and calling her name. It looks as if her dad is crying.

Standing at the bottom of it is Joe. He's applauding too. As she rides into the tunnel, she hears him shout, 'Great round, Ella. That was amazing.'

I beat him and he's congratulating me?

Turning in the saddle, she opens her mouth to reply, but he's already out of view.

CHAPTER FORTY-THREE

ELLA

At the final prize-giving of the show, the winners of the World Cup qualifier enter the international arena with Ella and Eagle's Crest at the front. Ella still can't believe they won. It seems like a dream and she keeps expecting to wake up, but she hasn't yet.

As Queen's 'We Are The Champions' plays over the loudspeakers, and the audience claps in time to the music, Ella steers Eagle's Crest towards the left side of the space she's been briefed to line up in. She halts the chestnut gelding beside one of the large flower arrangements and gives him a stroke on the neck. Eagle's Crest arches his head, clearly proud of himself.

To her right, Joe and Truckle Bay come to a halt, and the rest of the prize winners line up to his right. Ella sneaks a glance at Joe, but a particularly bright spotlight from the lighting rig above them refocuses onto her, its light dazzling. She blinks. She can't see Joe's face.

'Ella,' Joe says. 'I wanted to say I'm so—'

'And now to the prize-giving,' says the commentator, cutting him off.

Ahead of Ella, a group of elegantly dressed people are

approaching the line up. There's a couple in their forties – the man in a well-tailored suit and the woman in a long, burgundy dress – along with two young children, girls of maybe six and eight years old, both wearing pretty pink dresses.

'Presenting the prizes today are Mr Martin Stafford, the CEO of our title sponsor, along with his wife, Bernadette, and their two children, Sapphire and Ruby,' says the commentator. 'First to be presented are our winners – Ella Cooper and Eagle's Crest.'

Two stewards follow on behind the sponsor and his family. They both carry large wicker baskets, one containing rosettes and the other laden with carrots. As they approach Eagle's Crest, the chestnut gelding smacks his lips together, and Ella smiles.

'Someone's hungry,' says Bernadette Stafford, laughing. She turns to the tallest of the two young girls. 'Go ahead and feed him a carrot, Sapphire.'

The girl looks up at Ella shyly. 'Is it okay if I feed him?'

Ella nods encouragingly. 'Of course, he loves carrots.'

The girl approaches Eagle's Crest. She holds her palm flat with a carrot balanced on top. 'Here you are. Well done for winning.'

Eagle's Crest reaches out and gently takes the carrot from her hand then crunches it noisily, pieces of carrot falling from his mouth as he does so. The two little girls, Sapphire and Ruby, giggle with delight at his messy eating.

Ella grins and rubs the gelding's neck. 'Not too fast,' she warns him.

Martin and Bernadette Stafford wait until the carrot has been eaten before moving forward to present the prizes. Martin puts the winner's sash around Eagle's Crest's neck, and Bernadette hands Ella the winner's rosette and a silver trophy. Ella clips the rosette onto Eagle's Crest's bridle, and then poses with the family as the photographers take their picture. Eagle's Crest, who always loves having his photo taken, stands alert and proud with his ears pricked.

As the Staffords finish congratulating her and move on to present Joe with his prize, their smallest child, Ruby, grabs a carrot from the basket and rushes back to Eagle's Crest, her hand with the carrot outstretched.

The chestnut gelding is delighted to take another carrot and happily munches on his edible reward as the rest of the line-up are awarded their prizes.

After that, everything passes in a blur for Ella. She poses again for more photographs and then, before she's even had a chance to speak to Joe, it's time for the lap of honour.

As the commentator announces their names once again, Ella and Eagle's Crest lead the rest of the line-up in a canter around the arena. The audience clap, and over the loudspeakers, Katy Perry sings 'Firework'.

As they reach the exit, stewards wave Ella around the arena again for a solo lap.

The lights dim and a single spotlight illuminates them. The audience cheer louder as they clap their hands and stamp their feet. Ella's never experienced anything like it.

Turning down the centre of the arena, she relaxes her reins and lets Eagle's Crest step up a gear into gallop. As they fly across the arena, Ella crouches low over the gelding's neck and cries happy tears.

We've done it.

We won.

We're going to the World Cup.

CHAPTER FORTY-FOUR

HATTIE

It happens when she least expects it.

The World Cup qualifier prize-giving has just finished and Hattie leaves Daniel in the grandstands, watching the last Shetland Pony Grand National championship race and then the final dog agility championship, and nips back to the lorry to collect the things for Wayne's plan, and for Daniel and herself.

Out of the public areas, behind the scenes is a bustle of activity. Grooms are getting horses ready for the grand finale – tinsel is being threaded through plaits in the horses' manes and being sewn into tails – and the carriages are being prepared for the horses who will be pulling them during the show finale. There's still an hour to go until it's time, but there's an air of excitement and expectation. The London International Horse Show is coming to an end, and the finale is the last act of the week.

Pausing in the stables to feed The Rogue and Pink Fizz half a ginger biscuit each, Hattie checks both horses have enough hay and water, and continues on her way towards the lorry park. She's in the walkway when she hears footsteps behind her.

'Hattie?' calls a woman's voice.

She turns and sees Doug Wallingford's blonde groom, Pippa, rushing after her. 'What is it?'

Pippa stops and catches her breath. 'Look, I know this is a weird one, but Doug asked me to find you.'

'Doug?' Hattie can't hide the surprise in her voice. Given their last interaction, Hattie would've thought she was the last person Doug would want to see. 'Why?'

'It's about Arthur.'

Hattie thinks about the huge grey gelding and how Doug treated him earlier. Worry flutters in her chest. 'Is Arthur okay?'

'Yes, he's fine,' says Pippa, quickly. 'But Doug wants to sell him. He's sent me to ask if you're still interested in the horse, in buying him?'

'Doug must be really desperate if he's willing to let me have him,' says Hattie. Doug seemed so adamant before, that she'd be the last person he'd consider selling the horse to.

'He doesn't want to take Arthur home,' says Pippa, with sadness in her tone. 'Doug blames the horse for his suspension. Says he can't bear to look at him.'

Hattie thinks for a moment. Arthur's a big horse, probably too big for her really, but she felt such a strong connection to the grey gelding from the moment she met him. He's a sensitive horse who needs to be treated right. She can do that. And she's got the money left to her by her father squirrelled away in the bank account he set up for her. Surely removing Arthur from Doug's yard would be a good use for some of it?

I can't let him stay with Doug.

She looks at Pippa's hopeful face and nods. 'Of course I'll buy him. We've got space on our lorry; he can come home with us.'

Pippa's relief is clear from her expression. 'That's amazing. Thank you. He's such a good boy; Doug just never gave him a chance.'

'I saw that,' says Hattie, remembering how he treated the gelding. 'I'll do better by him.'

'I know you will,' says Pippa, beaming. 'Doug's in his lorry. Will you come now and make it official?'

'Sure,' says Hattie. 'Lead the way.'

Doug isn't so much hostile as seething when they meet. The price is a take it or leave it deal, and Hattie takes it even though she could never have imagined ever paying this much money for a horse, or for anything really. But it's worth it to get Arthur out of Doug's yard. With the bank transfer completed, Hattie leaves Doug's top-of-the-range six-horse lorry with Arthur's passport, microchip document, and a handwritten receipt and confirmation of transfer of ownership document.

'I'll sort his stable out once you've got him on your lorry,' says Pippa, falling into step beside Hattie. 'Don't worry about any of that.'

'Thank you,' replies Hattie. 'For this, and for caring about Arthur.'

'Of course,' says Pippa. 'And if you ever need another groom at Templeton Manor, please think of me. I'll give you my number in case you have any questions about Arthur. Stay in touch.'

Hattie smiles. 'I will.' She thinks for a moment. 'I'm going to need to get him a travel rug. What size is he?'

'Six foot nine,' says Pippa. 'He's a big guy.'

Hattie smiles. 'He's like the opposite of my mare. She's always the smallest at the competitions. Arthur's going to be one of the biggest.'

Pippa laughs. 'Do you think you'll take Arthur eventing?'

'I don't know,' says Hattie. 'I'll focus on gaining his trust and building a partnership, then we'll see what he likes to do.'

'Sounds perfect,' replies Pippa, her eyes becoming tearful. 'I'm so glad you're giving him a new home.'

They walk into the stable area and along the line towards

those assigned to Doug. In the furthest is Arthur. Unlike most of the other horses, the large grey gelding is standing at the back of his stable, his bottom propped up against the wall, snoozing.

He wakes as Pippa undoes the door bolt, and puts his ears forward in greeting. Hattie enters the stable. She holds her hand out, letting Arthur sniff her, then, as he lowers his head, gives him a scratch between his eyes. He leans into the scratch, and Hattie laughs.

'Is that good?' she says.

Arthur blows out.

Reaching into her pocket, she breaks off a small piece of ginger biscuit and offers it to him. He takes it tentatively. Chews. Then opens his mouth and spits the half-chewed biscuit onto the bedding.

'Okay, so you're not keen on that, huh?' says Hattie, smiling. 'Let's try this then.'

Reaching into her other pocket, Hattie removes a Polo from the packet she keeps there and offers it to Arthur. He sniffs the Polo suspiciously, checking it's not another piece of ginger biscuit. Then, realising that it isn't, he gently takes the mint from her palm.

'How's that?' asks Hattie, watching as the big gelding crunches on the Polo.

Arthur doesn't spit it out, which she takes as a good sign. Instead, he swallows the mint and then raises his top lip, showing his appreciation. Hattie laughs. 'So you're a Polo lover, are you? Excellent. I think you'll get on well with Mermaid.'

The big gelding nuzzles her pocket to confirm he would be very happy to receive another Polo, so Hattie obliges by feeding him a second one. 'You're coming home with us today,' she tells him, stroking his dappled neck as he chews happily. 'We're going to give you the best life.'

'When are you heading out?' asks Pippa from the other side of the stable door.

'After the finale,' Hattie tell her. She checks her watch and realises she's late for meeting Wayne. 'Speaking of which, I need to get going. Once the finale is done, I'll get Arthur some travelling stuff and come back here. I'll message you when I'm on my way.'

'Enjoy the finale,' says Pippa. 'It always looks so much fun.'

'Thanks,' says Hattie. 'I'm on a bit of a secret mission so I'd better hurry.'

'Sounds intriguing,' replies Pippa. 'Don't let me hold you up.'

Giving Arthur a final forehead rub, Hattie slips out of the stable door and hurries back towards the lorry park and the costumes and accessories she's collected that will help Wayne land his proposal. As she walks, she messages him quickly:

Sorry, I got held up. On my way. With you in 10.

Breaking into a jog, she weaves her way along the walkway and out to the lorry park. The big show finale is scheduled to start in twenty minutes.

I hope I'm not too late.

CHAPTER FORTY-FIVE

WAYNE

He was convinced this wasn't going to happen, but since Hattie turned up a couple of minutes ago, they've all done a quick change at the side of the warmup area and are now almost ready. Which is good, because Wayne can hear the steward shouting the five-minute warning.

'We need to line up in the collecting ring,' says Wayne, putting his elf hat on and making sure it's secure. 'Otherwise they'll think we're not coming.'

'It's okay,' says Megan, fitting the long, pointed elf shoes over the top of her boots. 'They can see we're here.'

'I don't know if they can,' says Wayne, doubtfully. The whole of the warmup and collecting ring area is full of people, horses and ponies ready to perform in the grand finale of the show. This version of it, as it is the last one of the show, has more people in it than on previous days, which is how Hattie managed to wangle them all a role. Some people, like the acrobats dressed as Christmas fairies, and the dancers dressed as gingerbread men, have choreographed roles, and others, like Hattie, Wayne and Megan, are there as 'extras' filling in as elves carrying presents to place in Santa's sleigh. Daniel's role is a bit different; he's been picked to ride in the carriage with the Ice Queen.

'Do you remember what we have to do?' asks Hattie.

'Carry a present, dance and make mischief?' says Megan, smirking. 'We are elves, after all.'

'True,' says Hattie, laughing. 'Aside from Daniel, of course.'

'I'd rather be an elf than wear this cravat,' says Daniel, grimacing as he puts his finger between his neck and the silk material of his white cravat, trying to loosen it. 'I have no idea why I was singled out to be a footman to the Ice Queen.'

'It'll be fun,' says Hattie. 'You get to ride in that cool carriage.'

They all look across towards where the carriages are lined up. The Ice Queen's is a delicate open-topped vehicle decorated in white and pale blue, giving it the appearance of being made from ice.

Daniel smiles. 'True. Although I think I'd rather be riding a horse than pulled by one; carriages always look rather wobbly.'

'Two minutes,' calls the steward. 'Take your places please, people.'

'Ready?' asks Wayne, feeling his stomach give a little lurch.

'Totally,' replies Megan, picking up her oversized Christmas present, wrapped like the others in gold shiny paper and a green ribbon. 'Let's do this.'

Wayne glances towards Hattie. She gives him an encouraging nod.

'Okay,' says Wayne, picking up his rectangular present.

'I'm right behind,' says Hattie. Turning to Daniel, she gives him a quick kiss. 'Have fun.'

'You too,' he says. 'See you afterwards.'

As Daniel heads across to the Ice Queen's carriage, Hattie follows Megan and Wayne across to the section of the collecting ring where the other elves are congregating.

Woah, thinks Wayne. There must be at least forty elves. The scale of this last finale is off the charts. There are so many other people milling around – at least the same numbers of fairies and gingerbread men, then all the people playing roles, like the Shetland pony rider who is playing the girl who forgot Christmas, and show jumping star Aimee Eastford who is playing her fairy godmother who shows her the magic of the season, and Santa Dog, played by a brown-and-white collie who's one of the dog agility champions. Then there are all the people riding their horses, all dressed in period costumes or fantasy creatures, and the carriages – the four-in-hand, the stagecoach, and the more delicate vehicles like the Ice Queen's. It really is an amazing sight.

'Quiet please,' calls the steward.

The lights dim in the international arena.

'And now it's time for our Christmas Finale,' announces the commentator. 'And it all starts with a young girl and her pony. The girl who forgot Christmas.'

As the music starts to play, the Shetland pony rider and her skewbald Shetland walk into the ring. The spotlight picks her out, a circle of light in the otherwise dark space, and as the narrator speaks and the performance begins, group by group they all start to move towards the arena, Wayne feels as if he's in a dream.

I can't believe I'm part of this.

Wayne touches his gloved hand to the pocket that Hattie has sown into the elf outfit for him, and feels the small box safely stowed there. His nerves flare.

I can't believe I'm going to do this.

CHAPTER FORTY-SIX

DANIEL

There's something unsettlingly sinister about the Ice Queen.

Daniel knows it's all special make-up effects, but with her ice-white skin, dark blue eyeshadow painted up to her eyebrows and frosted eyelashes and eyebrows, she looks more like a demon than a queen. As he climbs into the carriage and sits down beside her as instructed, Daniel feels suddenly uncomfortable.

'Hello again, Mr Templeton-Smith,' says the Ice Queen.

Daniel frowns. He knows that voice, but can't place where from. 'Erm... hi.'

The Ice Queen smiles. 'It's Candice. Candice Gladstone.' She pauses waiting for him to realise who she is, but he still can't place her. A frown flashes across her face before she banishes it. 'Arnold's wife. We presented the prizes to you and your team earlier.'

'Wow,' says Daniel – he hadn't expected that. 'What a transformation. Incredible.'

'Why, thank you,' says Candice, touching a gloved hand to her white-blonde hair that's piled high on her head and pinned in an elaborate twist, and checking her tiara, the shape of shards of ice, is still in position. 'It's always fun to dress up, isn't it.'

Daniel thinks about his still too-tight cravat and isn't sure he agrees, but he nods to be polite. 'Are you looking forward to this?'

'Very much so,' replies Candice, smoothing out the folds of the Ice Queen costume's skirt – multiple layers of blue-and-white organza and satin that cascade down from a tight, jewelled blue bodice. 'I do love to play a part.'

'Yours is a good one too,' says Daniel. The Ice Queen is the villain of the finale, the person responsible for casting the spell on the young girl to forget Christmas. She might get her come-uppance in the end, but it's a good role.

'My favourite,' says Candice, in her cut-glass accent.

There's something in the way she looks at him that makes Daniel's breath catch in his throat. He feels as if she's looked at him like that before, that they've been this close together before. It's a real déjà vu moment, but he has no idea why.

'One minute until the Ice Queen's entrance,' calls the steward, beckoning them over.

The carriage driver asks the two white horses pulling the carriage, resplendent in their jewelled bridles and white plumes, to walk forward to the entrance, ready to enter the arena through the tunnel.

'Isn't your husband joining us?' asks Daniel, looking around the collecting ring for Arnold T. Gladstone. There's still plenty of room in the carriage.

Candice shakes her head. She puts her hand on Daniel's thigh, her fingers pressing hard into his flesh, and says, 'No, darling. This isn't Arnold's sort of thing at all. He much prefers to watch.'

She holds his gaze, and Daniel feels himself blush. Did Candice Gladstone just come onto him? He has another sudden feeling of déjà vu.

The steward gives the carriage driver the sign to enter the arena, and the Ice Queen's entrance music begins to play. The horses leap into trot and pull them through the tunnel and into the spotlight.

As they thunder around the arena, Candice stands up in the carriage, arms outstretched, her Ice Queen wand in her right hand pointed directly at the little girl playing the girl who forgot Christmas, who is standing in the middle of the arena. She lets out an evil laugh and says to the child in an ice-tinged tone. 'Remember me?'

Daniel suddenly feels nauseous. Something is very wrong.

Why does Candice Gladstone seem so horribly familiar?

CHAPTER FORTY-SEVEN

JOE

He must find Ella. He can't let her leave without telling her he's sorry.

Nervously, Joe walks along the stables towards where Ella's two horses are housed. There's a lot of activity as grooms prepare the horses who aren't involved in the grand show finale to leave the showground, clear out their stables and set to work packing up all their equipment. He says hello to the people he recognises, and helps catch a falling blanket off the top of a pile of rugs being carried back towards the lorry park by Antonio's groom. The mood in the stables is light-hearted – like a 'last day of school' vibe – but Joe feels anything but that.

Up ahead, he sees Ella's parents are standing in the walkway, looking over the door into Eagle's Crest's stable. Ella must be in there. Hope flares inside him, then immediately his nerves intensify. He feels a bit sick.

I have to tell her.

He stops beside Ella's parents. 'Erm, hi, I'm looking for Ella.'

'She's in here,' says Ella's mum, gesturing towards the stable.

He looks over the stable door and sees Ella inside, rugging up Eagle's Crest.

Joe swallows hard. Forcing the courage to speak. 'Ella, I... Can we talk?'

She doesn't turn to look at him, concentrating instead on straightening up the chestnut gelding's rug and buckling the front straps into place. Joe sees that the stable has already been skipped out and all of Ella's equipment removed. The horse has his travel boots and tail guard on already. She must be almost ready to leave.

'Please, Ella, I...' Joe waits for her to turn to face him, but she doesn't.

'Shall we go and get some food for the drive back, love?' asks Ella's dad, glancing from Joe to Ella rather awkwardly.

'That'd be great, thanks, Dad,' says Ella, reaching underneath Eagle's Crest's belly and fastening the belly strap.

'Sandwiches and crisps?' says Ella's dad.

'And a chocolate bar to keep her strength up,' adds Ella's mum.

Still not looking towards Joe, Ella straightens up and smiles at her parents. 'Perfect.'

As her parents walk away towards the food trucks, Ella gives Eagle's Crest a stroke on his neck, then unbolts the stable door and steps out into the walkway. She looks at Joe, her expression unreadable. 'What do you want, Joe?'

This is it.

'I'm sorry,' says Joe. 'I was way out of line earlier.'

'Yes, you were,' agrees Ella evenly. 'I had things under control with Henry. I didn't need you to "save" me.'

'I know.' Joe looks down. Embarrassed. 'And I'm sorry I went off like that after the Santa Stakes.'

'Me too,' says Ella, pausing as Eagle's Crest sticks his head out over the stable door and starts nuzzling her coat pocket for a treat. 'I really liked you, Joe. I thought we'd connected but then—'

'I'm sorry, I just...' Joe stops. He takes a breath. 'I was an idiot. I got caught up in my thoughts, beating myself up for making an error and causing Pipplemouse to have the fence down. I didn't think… I should've come and congratulated you; instead I just wallowed in my own insecurities.'

'You should have talked to me,' says Ella, pulling a treat out of her pocket and feeding it to Eagle's Crest. 'It's not like you haven't seen me at my very worst, is it? I mean, *you* didn't even fall in the water.'

Joe nods, a smile twitching up the corners of his lips. 'I'm sorry.'

'So you've said,' replies Ella. Her voice turns more serious. 'I was hurt, Joe, really hurt. I didn't know what was going on. To me, it seemed like things were only good between us as long as you were winning and I stayed in my lane.'

Oh God.

'That's… No, I never meant to imply…' Joe shakes his head. How did he screw this up so badly? He's been such a fool. 'I was happy for you. I *am* happy, delighted for you. You won the bloody World Cup qualifier; that's utterly amazing.'

Ella stares back at him, saying nothing.

Around them, the grooms and other riders keep glancing over, clearly wondering what's going on. Joe usually hates to make any kind of a spectacle of himself, but right now he doesn't care. He just wants Ella to know how serious he is; what she means to him.

'*You're* amazing,' he continues. He has to tell her how he feels. Even if she blows him off, he must tell her. 'I've never felt for someone how I feel for you, Ella. We've barely known each other a week, but I can't imagine not having you in my life. I know I've blown it, but please give me another chance. I won't make you regret it.'

Ella holds his gaze for a long moment. 'You won't?'

Hope flares inside him. 'I promise.'

'You promise?' she says, cocking her head to the side. 'I will hold you to that.'

'I expect you to,' says Joe, smiling.

Ella nods. 'Okay, deal.'

Joe reaches for her hand. She steps closer, going up onto her tiptoes and kissing him. He pulls her closer. Inhaling the scent of her and kissing her deeply. Her fingers curl in his hair and the relief that she's forgiven him mingles with the feelings of love and desire that are cascading through him.

Someone nearby lets out a long whistle.

'Get a room,' calls another person, laughing.

Joe ignores them. He wants this kiss to last forever.

CHAPTER FORTY-EIGHT

CANDICE

The look on Daniel's face when she made that light come-on to him was priceless. Candice can tell he's confused – that he's thinking he knows her from somewhere, but just can't place where. He always was the most dreadful over-thinker, so it doesn't surprise her. It just makes the whole thing even more fun. She wonders how long it will be before he figures out how he knows her, and who she really is. Not long, she imagines, surely? She's given him enough clues.

It's hilarious, really. Part of her doesn't want to tell him, and the other part is desperate to blurt out the truth and see the horror on his face as the penny drops. Because she knows for sure that he will be horrified, and she is so here for it.

It's almost worth the discomfort of being pulled around in this bouncy, hard-seated carriage. Almost. Although, she has to admit, playing the part of the Ice Queen is proving rather a good laugh. After all, it's so much more preferable to be the villain than the hero, or so she's always thought. Villains always seem to have more fun.

It's coming to the end of her performance. The little girl

playing the lead character has just broken the curse that Candice's Ice Queen put on her and remembered Christmas after her fairy Godmother took her through a whistlestop tour of Christmases past and future – all acted out by various horse-and-rider stars. Now it's time for their big showdown.

The carriage bounces across the synthetic sand of the international arena towards the spot in the centre where the young girl is standing wearing her tinsel crown. As they approach her, Candice stands up in the carriage and flings her arms wide. 'You will never be free. I will curse you again and—'

'I am free,' says the girl, her young voice strong and confident. 'I remember what Christmas is. It's joy and hope and love. It's giving to others and sharing in a special time.'

The special effects team use lighting to create a bright light beam from the young girl to Candice's Ice Queen.

'No!' cries Candice, writhing as smoke starts to pour from her costume.

As the classical music reaches a triumphant crescendo, Candice slowly sinks down into the specially hollowed floor of the carriage, disappearing from the audience's sight as if she's melted into nothing.

The crowd cheers.

The young girl says, 'Merry Christmas, everyone.'

And as the music changes to Christmas songs, the Ice Queen's carriage moves out of the spotlight and towards the edge of the arena where they line up between the four-in-hand carriage and the stagecoach. Once they're in position, Candice gets out of her hiding place and sits back down on the hard wooden bench seat.

'Well done, that was great,' says Daniel.

'Thanks, Daniel,' says Candice. Except this time she doesn't use the posh accent she's been faking ever since she met Arnold T. Gladstone six months ago. No, this time she uses her own regular accent.

He stares at her, wide-eyed, like a rabbit in the headlights. It really is rather wonderful to see.

Candice smiles. 'What's the matter? You look like you've seen a ghost.'

'I... You just remind me of someone, and your voice...?'

'Do I?' says Candice, innocently. She's playing with him; she can't help it. After all, if it wasn't for him and that damn girl, Hattie, and that interfering old bag, Lady Pat, who seems to bankroll her, she'd still have her previous name, her previous home and her own fortune. She leans closer to Daniel. 'How's that, darling? Go on, tell me who it is that I remind you of.'

All the colour drains from Daniel's face. There's a tremble to his voice as he answers her in a hushed tone. 'Lexi Marchfield-Wright.'

Candice smiles wider. 'That's right, darling.'

Daniel jerks away as if she's just slapped him. Horror and confusion flash across his expression. 'Lexi? But you can't be... You look different, your hair's—'

'Poor naïve Daniel, you never change. Cosmetic surgery is very advanced these days, darling,' purrs Candice. 'When I realised the time was up on Dexter's property schemes, I did the smart thing. I emptied our bank accounts, took what I could pack into my suitcases, and left. Once I knew the police wanted to speak to me in connection with the fraudulent activities my husband was involved in, I realised I couldn't be Lexi Marchfield-Wright for a moment longer. So I got myself an excellent surgeon and had a bit of an upgrade,' she says, gesturing to her face. 'Then I bought myself a brand-new identity.'

Daniel stares back at her, speechless. The horror on his face is priceless. It's totally worth the risk of telling him. And it's strange: even though she remembers just how unsatisfactory he was in bed, she still wants to fuck him. Who knows why; maybe it's just to prove that she can.

The Christmas songs have faded, and now all around them,

performers and the audience have joined hands and voices to sing 'Auld Lang Syne'. Candice offers Daniel her gloved hand, and he shrinks away to the farthest corner of the bench seat.

'Don't touch me,' he says, pushing her hand away. 'Keep away from me and from Hattie. After what you did, I can't believe you'd have the audacity to come back here. You're still wanted by the police.'

Candice cocks her head to the side. Same Daniel, always making such a drama about things. As she observes him and his discomfort, Santa's sleigh, pulled by two white ponies, travels around the outside of the arena and faux snow starts to fall from the rafters above them. The audience starts to clap and cheer as Santa and his team of elves throw presents into the grandstands. The finale, and her private time with Daniel, is almost over. She feels almost sad about it.

'Where's your Christmas cheer, darling?' asks Candice, batting her eyelashes at Daniel. 'Isn't forgiveness a bit of a theme for this time of year?'

'What you did was unforgivable,' says Daniel, and she can see that he means it from the anger in his eyes and the rigid set of his jaw. 'You should be in jail with your husband.'

'Merry Christmas, everyone,' says the commentator. 'And a Happy New Year and safe journey home to you all.'

The driver asks the horses pulling their carriage to trot on, and they follow the path of the stagecoach in a final lap around the arena towards the exit. Waving to the audience with one hand, Candice moves along the bench seat until she's as close as she can get to Daniel.

He shivers. It's as if she really is an Ice Queen.

'Don't get any stupid ideas into your head, darling,' says Candice. 'If you tell anyone about my true identity, I'll tell the world about what you did for money last year, and just how your eventing exploits were funded. I'm sure the tabloids would love to know *that* story about this year's Badminton winner, wouldn't they?' She giggles. 'Just think of all the juicy stories I could tell them.'

Daniel's cheeks flush red. 'Why would you—'

'Because, darling...' Candice narrows her eyes and holds his gaze with a deadly serious stare. 'I still own you. Never forget that.'

CHAPTER FORTY-NINE

WAYNE

The faux snow is falling. This is the moment. It has to be now.

With his heart pounding in his chest so hard it feels like it might burst out at any moment, Wayne looks into Megan's eyes and takes her hand. 'Megan?'

She smiles, and in that moment she's never looked more beautiful. Even in her elf costume with the comical hat and overly long and pointed shoe covers, she looks like a million dollars. Wayne so wants to do this. He's also terrified. He never imagined he'd have a steady girlfriend, let alone make a permanent commitment to them. Until earlier this year, he was happy as a bachelor boy about town; now he can't imagine life without Megan.

He swallows down his nerves. Takes a deep breath.

Here goes.

Wayne sinks down onto one knee.

Megan's eyes widen. 'What are you—'

'I've got something to ask you,' says Wayne, trying to stop the nerves from affecting his voice.

Megan bites her lower lip. She sounds as nervous as he's feeling. 'Okay.'

The faux snow swirls around the pair of them and 'We Wish You A Merry Christmas' starts to play as the performers, horses and riders and carriages from the show finale form a procession and start a lap around the edge of the arena.

Fumbling in his pocket, Wayne pulls out the ring box. He lets go of Megan's hand for a moment and opens the box, holding it out towards her. 'I love you more than anything, Megan. Please say you'll spend the rest of your life with me.'

Megan's surprise is clear on her face. She puts a hand to her chest. 'Wayne, I…'

That's when the spotlight hits them, flooding the area around them with bright white light.

'And what's this?' says the commentator. 'Do we have a Christmas proposal taking place between two of Santa's elves? I think we do.'

There are *ooooh*s from the audience. Everyone in the grandstands is now looking at them. This wasn't the plan. Wayne thought he'd be able to do it without attracting attention. Now he realises his plan was flawed.

No pressure then.

Wayne's heart rate accelerates. Megan still hasn't answered.

What if she says no? Please don't let her say no.

He can't hide the nerves from his voice now. 'Megan, did you—'

'Yes, of course, yes,' says Megan, nodding vigorously. 'Yes, yes, yes.'

'That's amazing,' says Wayne, jumping to his feet. Taking the ring from the box, he removes Megan's elf glove and slips the ring onto her finger. He pulls her into his arms. 'Thank you. Oh my God, that's the scariest thing I've ever done.'

'Did you think I'd say no?' says Megan, laughing. 'I can't think of anything I want more than to be with you.'

Leaning forward, she kisses him.

As 'We Wish You A Merry Christmas' plays on, the faux snow continues to fall, and the thousands of spectators in the grandstands clap and cheer, Wayne kisses Megan. He feels like the luckiest man alive.

CHAPTER FIFTY

HATTIE

Daniel's been really quiet the whole drive home. He's tired from the week of competition, Hattie gets that, but he's had a permanent frown on his face since they took part in the show finale earlier this afternoon, and she doesn't get why.

It's already dark as they pull off the road into the driveway to Templeton Manor. As they wait for the automatic gates to open, Hattie glances across at Daniel. 'Are you okay?'

'Sure,' says Daniel, but he doesn't look it.

'Are you?' asks Hattie. 'You seem preoccupied.'

Daniel turns towards her. There's worry etched across his brow. 'It's… I'm just…' He shakes his head. Up ahead, the manor's wrought iron gates have fully opened. He gestures towards the driveway. 'Let's get the horses settled, yeah?'

'Okay,' says Hattie, frowning herself now. Daniel's clearly not happy, but she has no idea why. He was on such a high after winning the eventers vs show jumpers competition, she just doesn't get what's changed and that worries her. They talk about everything and anything. Sure, back in the earlier days they had some secrets from each other – the deal Daniel had made with the awful Lexi Marchfield-Wright last year for one, and even until this autumn, Hattie had kept the huge amount of money she'd been left by her father from Daniel, unable to tell him about it until she'd processed the surprise news herself. But since then, they've shared everything. Now it feels as if Daniel's holding something back.

'Okay,' says Hattie, nodding. 'But once the horses are done, we need to talk.'

Daniel reaches out and takes her hand, giving it a squeeze. 'Yes, we do.'

~

As they drive into the parking area beside the yard, Hattie tries to push away the fear that's building in her chest. She hates not knowing what's bothering Daniel. Is it something about her or the horses? Or have the money worries he's been fighting the past couple of years suddenly worsened? She wishes they could talk about whatever it is right now.

But they can't. Because Eddie, Daniel's head groom, and Jenny, the local vet and Eddie's fiancé, are rushing out of the manor house towards them, swiftly followed by McQueen, Eddie's three-legged collie, Popsy, Jenny's young cocker spaniel, and Poppet, Popsy's brother, who belongs to Hattie.

Hattie's heart lifts when she sees her little red dog hurtling towards her. Climbing out of the cab, she holds her arms out wide and the young spaniel throws himself into them. She hugs his wiggling furry body tight, laughing as he frantically licks her face. 'I missed you too, baby.'

'Welcome back,' says Eddie.

'It's good you're home already,' says Jenny. 'They've forecast snow tonight.'

'It feels cold enough,' says Hattie, shivering now she's out of the heated cab. 'It's far colder here than it was in London.'

'Congratulations, Daniel,' says Eddie, as Daniel joins them.

'Thanks,' he says.

Eddie, picking up on Daniel's mood, glances across at Hattie. She shrugs. Eddie has worked with him for many years. He knows as well as she does that when Daniel goes quiet, there's something major bothering him.

'We'd better get the horses off the lorry,' says Daniel, putting a bit more enthusiasm into his voice. 'Once they're settled, dinner and a few drinks sound good. We can unpack the lorry tomorrow. I'm knackered. Shall we get a takeaway?'

'Good plan,' says Jenny. 'You guys sort the horses, and I'll give the pizza place a call. Sound good?'

'Perfect,' says Daniel, smiling gratefully. 'You're a lifesaver.'

Laughing, Jenny heads back to the manor with Popsy scampering along behind her.

As they walk round to the rear of the lorry and undo the ramp, Daniel seems in better spirits. *Maybe he is just tired,* thinks Hattie, but she's not convinced. If he wants to talk, there's definitely something behind his sombre mood on the journey home. She just wants to know what it is.

Right now, she needs to focus on Arthur, though. Hattie turns to Eddie. 'We've brought home a bit of a surprise.'

'Oh yes?' replies Eddie. 'What?'

Daniel pulls the lorry's ramp down and Arthur's grey face looks out over the ramp gates. He looks around at his new surroundings, ears pricked.

'Who's this?' says Eddie. He looks at Daniel. 'You brought home a new horse?'

'Not me,' says Daniel, laughing. He points towards Hattie.

'How? Who?' asks Eddie. 'I want to know everything.'

'Let's just say Arthur wasn't getting on with his rider,' says Hattie, shrugging.

Eddie's eyes widen. 'Is this Arthur V? The horse Doug Wallingford was riding? We saw that fall he had from him. I said to Jenny they were clearly a bad match but Doug's behaviour was so out of line. I'm glad he got suspended.'

'Me too,' agrees Hattie, nodding. 'Arthur is a sweetheart, but he's a sensitive soul and Doug treated him badly. He was so rough, it was excruciating to watch.' She shudders. 'But Arthur's here now.'

'So what's the plan with him? Is he here for training, or to sell?'

'He's mine,' says Hattie, smiling. 'I bought him.'

Eddie's silent for a moment, no doubt working out how much money Arthur, as an international-level show jumper, would've cost. He doesn't say that, though; he's more tactful. Instead, he simply says, 'Congratulations.'

Hattie smiles. 'Thanks. I'm hoping in time that he might fancy a bit of eventing, but we'll see.'

'Hattie had a brief ride on him in London and they got on famously,' says Daniel, reaching out and giving Hattie's arm a squeeze. 'I'm pretty sure, whatever you do, Arthur's going to be happy here.'

Arthur whinnies as if to agree. Across through the darkness in the back field, Mermaid's Gold answers him.

Hattie smiles. She hopes the two of them will be friends.

As Eddie hurries off to prepare a stable for Arthur, Hattie heads up the ramp and unbolts the ramp gates. It's a tight space but, although a big horse, Arthur takes care not to squash her as she unties his lead rope. Daniel moves the ramp gates aside, and Hattie leads Arthur down the ramp and into the stable yard.

She puts her hand on the grey gelding's neck. 'Welcome to your new home, Arthur.'

Half an hour later, Arthur, The Rogue and Pink Fizz are all happily settled in their stables, have had their dinner, and are contently tucking into their hay. Eddie has moved the tack from the lorry to the tack room, but aside from that, they're leaving the unpacking until tomorrow.

'Pizza's here,' calls Jenny from the back porch of the manor house. 'Drinks too.'

'That sounds good,' says Eddie, striding across the yard towards the house, an enthusiastic McQueen, who's always partial to a bit of pizza, hurrying after him.

Daniel closes the yard gate and falls in step with Hattie. Poppet, who has stuck like Velcro to her since they arrived back, remains at her side.

As they walk towards the manor, their breath rising in clouds in the frigid air, Hattie feels the first flakes of snow land on her face. It's real snow this time, not the fake stuff from the finale. Still, fake or not, it looked perfect as Wayne proposed to Megan in the middle of the international arena. There's never been a show finale like it, and the cheers the audience gave the newly engaged couple were really something. Hattie's so pleased she was able to help Wayne make it happen.

But now Daniel's looked grim-faced again, and she can't let whatever's going on with him stay unspoken. She puts her hand on his arm. 'Danny?'

He stops and meets her gaze. Nods. 'I know. We need to talk.'

'So tell me, what's bothering you?'

Daniel takes a deep breath. Looks into her eyes.

And then he tells her.

JUST OVER TWO WEEKS LATER

CHAPTER FIFTY-ONE

DANIEL

It's eight o'clock on New Year's Eve and the party is just getting started. They've cranked the rather obstinate heating system up to the max and decorated the downstairs reception rooms with twinkling fairy lights and evergreen foliage. Even with the light dusting of snow and the rather bitter wind outside, the inside of Templeton Manor is warm and cosy.

Daniel glances over at Hattie, who is bent over, peering into one of the Aga's ovens at a batch of mini salmon en croutes. 'How are they looking?'

'Almost done,' says Hattie, closing the Aga's door and straightening up. 'Just a couple more minutes. We can start taking the rest of the stuff, though.'

'Great,' says Daniel. 'That'll keep the troops happy.'

New Year's Eve isn't a formal dinner, but they've spent the afternoon preparing a range of buffet-style dishes for people to help themselves to. With most of the horses turned away on their winter break, there's not as much to do in the stables and he's been enjoying having more time to experiment in the kitchen as well as helping Eddie and Bunty with stable yard maintenance, and some paddock fencing and field shelter repairs.

Hattie loads a tray with hummus, salsa and baba ghanoush, along with crudites, cheese twists, sourdough thins and sweet chilli crisps. She passes it to Daniel. 'Here you go. Lead the way, I'll bring the salads.'

They walk to the dining room where the formal table is already prepared with a white tablecloth, a pile of plates, cutlery and napkins. They set down the food, then head back to the kitchen for more.

It takes a few trips to ferry all the food to the table. There are vegetable quiches and mini roast potatoes, tiny beef wellingtons and cocktail sausages, cranberry-and-brie filo parcels, a cheese board, freshly baked sourdough bread, along with a large selection of vegan dishes.

'Do you think we've got enough?' asks Hattie, raising her eyebrow.

Daniel smiles. 'I might have over-catered a bit.'

'You think?' she says, laughing. She leans across and kisses him. 'It's perfect.'

Daniel feels a burst of pride. 'Thanks.'

'I need to fetch the salmon in a minute, but shall we tell the hordes that the food's ready?'

'Let's do it,' says Daniel.

Hand in hand, they walk towards the lounge where their friends have been having drinks. As they open the door, Poppet leaps up from where he'd been sprawled out in front of the fire and hurtles across the room to Hattie. She bends down, stroking the enthusiastic young spaniel, who is dancing around her feet in delight.

'Ah, there they are,' says Lady Pat. 'We wondered where you two had got to.'

'You're about to see,' says Daniel. 'Dinner is served.'

'How wonderful,' says Lady Pat, clapping her hands together. 'I'm famished.'

Dinner goes down well. They eat with plates on their knees in the lounge like the slap-up New Year's Eve suppers Daniel remembers from when he was a child. Lady Pat and Gerald sit on two of the dining chairs brought into the room for extra seating, Lady Pat saying her back much prefers a firmer chair to the sofa these days.

Hattie's best friend, Liberty, and her partner, the music legend JaXX, sit on the two-seater loveseat, feasting on the vegan dishes and telling Daniel how impressed they are with his mini mushroom pies. Megan and Wayne have been getting wedding planning tips from Eddie and Jenny. Daniel can't believe that Eddie and Jenny's wedding is less than a year away already, and from the conversation it sounds as though Megan and Wayne are thinking about planning theirs for next year too. Daniel's working pupil, Bunty, and her partner, local farmer Tom, sit on two of the footstools, surrounded by the dogs. McQueen, ever the gentleman, waits patiently for the humans to finish, but the two young cocker spaniels sit staring at poor Bunty and Tom, willing them to drop a morsel of food for them to hoover up. Gertrude, Daniel's small black cat who rules over the dogs, sits on the back of Daniel's wingback armchair, pretending to doze but ready to pounce if any salmon falls to the ground.

Hattie sits on the other wingback armchair to eat hers. Daniel makes sure that people's glasses are topped up. He doesn't have much of an appetite, he hasn't done since his encounter with Lexi Marchfield-Wright, or Candice Gladstone as she's now calling herself, at the finale of London International Horse Show.

'We did a good job,' says Hattie, as Gerald, the last to finish eating, puts his knife and fork down. 'Shall we clear the plates and get pudding?'

'Good idea,' says Daniel, rising to his feet.

They collect up the plates and head back to the kitchen. As

Hattie gets the puddings ready, Daniel takes the whipping cream from the fridge, pours it into a bowl and gets to work.

As he whips the cream, he suddenly feels exhausted. Since he learnt who Candice Gladstone really was, he's been struggling to sleep. It seems so wrong that, after what she and her husband did – stealing all those people's money – she can just change her name and waltz back into another privileged life without a care in the world.

Hattie is the only person he's told, and she was as shocked as he'd been. They've talked about it a few times, but Daniel hasn't been able to decide what to do. He wants to tell the police about Lexi's new identity – it's the right thing to do; she's wanted for questioning by them. But if he does that, she's threatened to tell all about what he did last year – how he'd accepted a deal to ride her horses and also to service her, for money.

Daniel shakes his head. He's just made it onto the list of potential riders for the British team at the next Olympics. If Lexi made good on her threat and told the media about their deal, a scandal like that would mean he'd have to step aside. He couldn't bring the team, the country, into disrepute. He just couldn't.

So what should he do?

'Penny for them,' says Hattie, putting her hand on his arm. 'I think that cream is well and truly whipped.'

He turns to face her.

She frowns. 'Daniel, are you okay?'

'It's the Lexi thing,' he says. 'I can't get it out of my head.'

Hattie puts her arms around him. 'I know,' she says gently. 'You need to make a decision.'

'Yeah.' Daniel pulls her closer. He strokes her hair. 'I'm sorry that—'

'You have nothing to be sorry for,' says Hattie fiercely. 'What that woman did was wrong, and then to threaten to use it against you… It makes me so furious.'

'Me too,' says Daniel. 'She can't be allowed to get away with swindling all those honest people out of their savings. I can't have her never being caught on my conscience.'

Hattie nods. 'I agree.'

'Thanks,' says Daniel. He puts the bowl of whipped cream onto the tray Hattie's set out with mini chocolate puddings and individual apple pies. 'Can you take this through? I'll join you in a moment. I have to do something first.'

Hattie nods. 'Whatever happens, whatever that woman does or says, we'll get through it. We'll face it together.'

Daniel watches as Hattie picks up the pudding tray and carries it through to the lounge, then walks across to where his phone is charging. He has to do the right thing, whatever the personal cost, and he doesn't want to see in the new year still harbouring this secret.

Taking a breath, Daniel picks up his phone and dials the non-emergency police number. The call connects and he feels his heart rate accelerate.

This is it.

The call handlers asks him how they can help.

There's no going back.

Daniel clears his throat, then says clearly, 'I'd like to report a sighting of a wanted fugitive. Her name's Lexi Marchfield-Wright but she's now going by Candice Gladstone.'

He gives the police all the information he knows, then hangs up. Putting his phone back on charge, Daniel exhales. Relief at having done something – told the police – floods through him. Whatever happens, he's done the right thing, and that's all he can do.

If Lexi makes their agreement public, he'll deal with it. He and Hattie will face it together. He feels so lucky to have found Hattie. He refuses to waste a moment longer worrying about what-ifs.

Striding through to the lounge, he pulls Hattie into his arms and kisses her. 'I love you,' he whispers into her ear.

Their friends whoop and cheer.

'Get a room,' calls Bunty, laughing.

Poppet, keen to get a cuddle too, jumps up, scrabbling at Daniel's and Hattie's legs. They laugh, and Hattie scoops the young dog into her arms and kisses him on his silky red head.

'Are you ready to dance?' says Daniel, reaching for the light switch and dimming the lights.

Hattie turns the music on, along with the disco lights she's fixed to the top of the wall units, and the room transforms into a dance floor. Daniel and Hattie start to dance and their friends join them.

With Hattie in his arms, good music playing and his friends around him, Daniel feels suddenly lighter, and happier, than he's felt since his encounter with Lexi Marchfield-Wright.

Who knows what the next year will bring. But tonight, he's going to have fun.

AFTERWORD

Firstly, I'd like to thank you, the reader, for reading this book. I really hope you enjoyed this third book in the Leightonshire Lovers series as much as I enjoyed writing it. Please let me know your thoughts by posting a review on Amazon; it would really mean a lot.

Getting a book prepared for publication takes a brilliant team. I'd like to say a huge thank you to the fabulous author Ed James for mentoring me through the process, to John Rickards, excellent copyediting guru, to Victoria Goldman, brilliant eagle-eyed proofreader, and the amazingly creative Louise Brown for the cover design – you are all awesome. A big shout out to my family and friends for all your support and encouragement, and of course to the horses who have been such huge parts of my life – Piglet, Floppy, Bertie, Mouse, Snout, Turt, Molly, Daisy, Libby, Holly and, of course, Parsley, with whom it all began.

If you'd like to find out more about me, you can hop over to my website at www.joniharperwriter.com and check out my socials via Instagram @joniharperwriter or Facebook @joniharperwriter – it's always great to connect.

You can also stay up to date on my book news by signing up to my Readers Club – turn the page to find out more!

Until next time…

Joni x

THE CHASE

A FREE LEIGHTONSHIRE LOVERS SHORT STORY

Join the Joni Harper Readers Club and get access to THE CHASE – a free short story set in and around Leightonshire and the equestrian world.

I've also included a bonus short story along with it – THE TROT UP.

As a member of the Readers Club you'll receive book and writing news updates and have the opportunity to enter exclusive giveaways. It's all completely free and you can opt out at any time.

To join, follow this link **joniharperwriter.com** and click on **Join My Readers' Club**.

GRIT & GLAMOUR

LEIGHTONSHIRE LOVERS SERIES BOOK ONE

Horse whisperer Hattie Kimble dreams of winning the prestigious Badminton Horse Trials and representing Great Britain at the Olympics, but without a job or a horse she's further from her goal than ever. When she takes a housesitting assignment in Leightonshire county – right in the heart of horse country – her luck begins to change and she's asked to work with a talented event horse who has lost her trust in humans. Hattie wasn't looking for love but when she meets Daniel Templeton-Smith at her first horse trials she can't deny the instant attraction. Should she follow her dream or her heart, or can she do both?

Event rider Daniel Templeton-Smith is broke. When he can't see any other way to pay the bills for crumbling Templeton Manor, he accepts an offer from alpha female Lexi Marchfield-Wright that involves more than just riding horses. As his career takes off, and he meets and starts falling for Hattie Kimble, he realises the price of success might be too high. But Lexi won't let him break their arrangement, and sets out to sabotage the developing relationship between Daniel and Hattie, whatever it takes.

GRIT & GLAMOUR is a spicy, adrenaline-fuelled equestrian sports romance set in the rural idyll of Leightonshire county and the high-octane world of eventing. Feelings grow and hearts are shattered, promises are made and friends are double-crossed, and as emotions reach breaking point, feuds erupt at the end-of-season winter ball, with devastating consequences.

https://mybook.to/PUVaD

ENVY & ELEGANCE

LEIGHTONSHIRE LOVERS SERIES BOOK TWO

Event riders Hattie Kimble and Daniel Templeton-Smith are falling for each other, but Hattie is hiding a secret from Daniel and as the weeks pass telling him the truth seems to get harder than ever. As the eventing season throws them challenge after challenge, will Hattie and Daniel's relationship grow stronger or is it going to break apart?

Farrier Wayne Jefferies is living the dream. Fresh from his appearance in the Rural Pleasures charity calendar, he's had more one-night stands than he can count, but when he meets aspiring dressage rider Megan Taylor he starts to experience something he's never felt before – love. If only she felt the same way.

Megan Taylor can barely make ends meet, so when her tack is stolen and she can't afford to replace it, she starts a side-hustle on OnlyFans. The money starts pouring in, but it's not long before she's attracting unwanted attention that threatens to destroy her job, her friendships and her budding equestrian career. The one man she's interested in seems to have friend-zoned her. Can she get him to change his mind?

Dressage diva Jem Baulman-Carter becomes an Instagram sensation when she posts a video of herself crying after her tack room is burgled. But when Daniel Templeton-Smith turns down her romantic advances, she vows to get her revenge on him.

ENVY & ELEGANCE is a spicy, adrenaline-fuelled equestrian sports romance set in the rural idyll of Leightonshire county and the interconnected worlds of eventing and dressage.

https://mybook.to/SI6Uuqz

ABOUT THE AUTHOR

Joni Harper began riding horses almost as soon as she could walk and started her competitive horse riding career aged six years old. She was a keen member of the Pony Club and as an adult rode successfully for many years in British Eventing competitions. She's been a Pony Club instructor in the UK, a Riding Counsellor in the USA, and has mucked out more stables than she can possibly count. She also trained as a horse whisperer. Joni has an MA in Creative Writing and loves to write about horses, the countryside and goings on in rural communities.

Printed in Great Britain
by Amazon

53478203R00153